I TOTALLY FUNNIEST

A MIDDLE SCHOOL STORY

JAMES PATTERSON

and CHRIS GRABENSTEIN

ILLUSTRATED BY LAURA PARK

SCHOLASTIC INC.

ISBN 978-0-545-84815-2

12 11 10 9 8 7 6 5 4 3 2 1   15 16 17 18 19 20/0

Printed in the U.S.A.   40

First Scholastic paperback printing, September 2015

For Serena Wetmore,
Jamie's biggest fan
—JP

PART ONE

Finally, the Finals!

Chapter 1

START THE COUNTDOWN CLOCK

Hi! I'm Jamie Grimm, and it's great to be back in front of an audience. This way, when I die in three days, at least I won't be alone.

Let me explain.

I've won a few rounds in something called the Planet's Funniest Kid Comic Contest—the local, state, regional, and semifinal competitions. Now, in three days, I'll be in THE FINALS out in Hollywood.

I'm trying my best not to freak out.

Unfortunately, everybody keeps reminding me of my impending doom.

My friends at school.

The cafeteria lady.

Teachers, strangers—even the billboards in Times Square!

My whole life has become this wild NCAA tournament of comedy. I've made it past the Sweet Sixteen all the way to the Elite Eight, where I'm hoping for a shot at the Final Four.

Oh, in case you haven't heard, that shot comes in THREE DAYS.

But don't worry—even if you don't live in the Los Angeles area, you can watch me die. Live. On cable TV's YUX channel.

By the way, *dying onstage* is what comedians call it when they flop, tank, or bomb so badly they're blasted with boos and pelted with week-old produce. It's what I'll probably be doing in, oh, maybe THREE DAYS!

So cue the Olympic fanfare music.

It all comes down to this, like they say on ESPN. It's now or never. Do or die. This is for all the marbles, even though nobody actually plays marbles anymore. In three days, there will be no tomorrow, so who cares about the four-day forecast?

Yep. This comedy gig is about to get super-serious. And, like I said, for this final Hollywood round, there are only eight of us still standing.

Actually, the seven other kids will be doing all

the standing. Me? Not so much.

In case you haven't noticed, I'm a stand-up comedian who doesn't exactly fit the job description.

Chapter 2

SMILEYVILLE:
THE TOWN WITH THE FROWN

Meet the Smileys.

That's what I call my aunt, uncle, and cousins.
I've been living with them in Long Beach, a suburb
of New York City, ever since I left the rehab hospital
I went to after the horrible car accident. The crash
where I lost my parents and sister, not to mention
the use of my legs, feet, and toes.

See how excited the Smileys are about the big
comedy contest coming in three days? Believe me,
for them, this is excited.

"Be sure you pack an extra pair of clean
underwear for Hollywood," says Mrs. Smiley.

"And a toothbrush," adds Mr. Smiley. "But don't

roll it up in your extra pair of underwear. I did that once and regretted my decision later."

Have you noticed that the Smileys don't smile very much? That's why I call them that. Even their dog, Ol' Smiler, is gloomy. The last time he wagged his tail, it was to swat a fly.

Trust me, we're not smiling on the inside, either.

I roll out of my bedroom in the Smileys' garage (it's where they park all the stuff with wheels— lawn mower, wheelbarrow, snowblower, me) and head off to school. Since it's pretty early in the morning, the sidewalks are full of dogs walking their people.

Oh, sure—you might think the people are walking the dogs, but that's not the way I see it.

Come on, if two creatures are walking side by side and one is picking up the other's poop, who do you think is in charge?

The leash? That's how dogs make sure their humans don't wander away.

I'm actually thinking about getting some dogs. Alaskan Malamutes. Six of 'em. They make such excellent sled dogs, I figure I could get to school a whole lot faster if I hooked up a sled team and yelled, "Mush!" Of course, with six dogs I'd probably need to carry a jumbo-sized pooper scooper.

A couple of the dogs give me a sniff when I roll by, but most of the people are so well trained, they don't even notice me.

I'm sort of the Invisible Kid on the streets of Long Beach, where no one seems to be all that excited about the big comedy contest on cable TV in less than THREE DAYS!

But at school, things are different.

Way different.

Chapter 3

MIDDLE SCHOOL COOL? ME?

OMG!" screeches this very cute girl who I think is (or should be) a cheerleader. "It's Jamie Grimm!"

Now all her friends start squealing, shrieking, and screaking. I half-expect the glass in the trophy case to shatter when one of their wails hits a note so high even Ol' Smiler couldn't hear it.

"Have you really met Judy Nazemetz?" asks a swooning fan.

Not one of *my* fans. This girl is crazy about Judy Nazemetz, another of the eight kid comics competing in the finals. Judy's very nice and incredibly funny and already stars in her own Disney Channel sitcom called *Judy, Judy, Judy!*

"Yeah," I say. "We've been friends since the New York round of the competition."

"Do you know Ben, too?" gushes another girl, batting her eyes.

Ben Baccaro is another comic in the Elite Eight. Maybe sixteen years old, Ben calls himself the Italian Scallion and always wears a tight white tee that shows off his bulging chest muscles, which, by the way, he wiggles badda-bing style every time he cracks a joke.

"I haven't met Ben," I say. "Not yet. But he'll be out in Hollywood with me."

And then I go deaf. Because two dozen girls scream in my ears.

Even my old comic nemesis Vincent O'Neil, who used to tell everybody he was "a bazillion times funnier than Jamie Grimm," is now a fan.

"Here's a joke you can borrow for Hollywood," he says when we bump into each other in the hall.

"Thanks, Vincent, but—"

"So, how do you make a tissue dance?"

I cringe a bit. "Put a little boogey in it?"

"Oh, you already have that one. Excellent. Here's another."

"Um, I'm really not doing joke book jokes anymore, Vincent. I'm trying to stick with observational—"

"What did Winnie-the-Pooh say to his agent?"

Okay. This one I don't know. So I shrug.

"Show me the honey!" booms Vincent. Now I wish I could un-know it. "Get it? 'Show me the honey!' Because usually movie stars say 'Show me the money' to their agent, but since Pooh is a bear..."

"Right. Got it. Thanks."

"Feel free to use it. You don't even have to split the one hundred thousand dollars with me when you win."

Did I forget to mention that?

The grand-prize winner of the Planet's Funniest Kid Comic Contest will take home a check for one hundred thousand dollars.

In less than three days!

Chapter 1

MY BESTIES
(FRIENDS, NOT JOKES)

Now, if you ever hung out with me at school, you'd know my best friends are Gilda Gold, Joey Gaynor, and Jimmy Pierce.

Gilda's gutsy, smart, and funny. Knows more about classic comedians than even I do.

Check out my Groucho Marx impression: "I find television very educational. Every time someone switches it on, I go into another room and read a good book."

Gaynor? He's a little edgier than most middle school kids—even the other ones with nose rings.

And Pierce is a total brainiac. He knows everything, including the fact that it's physically impossible for pigs to look up at the sky, so they'll never know when one of their pals is flying.

These three have been my buds through thick and thin and then thick again and then some more thin and then extra-thick. It's kind of like we're a pack of bacon.

But lately...

Well, I haven't really had all that much time to hang with my friends. I've been, you know, busy. Working on new material. Packing all that clean underwear for the trip out to California. Wincing at cute cheerleaders squealing in my ears.

Basically being a big shot.

But for all the attention it's gotten me, I've been thinking that this comedy gig was a lot more fun back when I was just cracking up Gilda, Gaynor, and Pierce around the losers' table in the school cafeteria.

Back then there weren't any contests or ginormous cardboard checks to cash.

Back then it was just fun being funny.

Is it weird to miss the "good old days" when they were only, like, a couple of weeks ago?

Maybe there is such a thing as too much fun. It's kind of like too much ice cream. It feels great when you're scarfing it down. Later, you feel kind of queasy.

That's what this is like.

Kind of queasy.

But I keep scarfing it down.

Chapter 5

CRAMMING FOR THE FINALS

But, like I said, I don't really have time to worry about missing my friends.

That countdown clock keeps on ticking.

After school, I zip down the boardwalk to my uncle Frankie's diner to do my homework. Not for algebra or science—for Comedy 101.

I'm cramming for The Finals the way most kids cram for finals.

Uncle Frankie was the one who first suggested that I sign up for the comedy contest. He saw me cracking up his customers when I worked the cash register after school and on weekends. Back then I had a lot of jokes rattling around inside my head, because when I was in the rehab hospital after the accident, the doctors and nurses lent me all sorts of joke books and comedy videos. They all told me "Laughter is the best medicine." Unless you have toe fungus. Then you should really ask for an ointment.

Anyway, I think I memorized every classic comedy bit ever done. So, if a customer had a special request, I was always happy to oblige.

By the way, my uncle Frankie is an excellent comedy coach. After all, he knows a thing or two about competitions. He used to be the yo-yo champion of Brooklyn and made it all the way to the World Yo-Yo Olympics, where he won a gold medal. It was on a string so he could twirl it.

To help me get into "the zone," Uncle Frankie—
who has finals fever even worse than I do—has
totally redecorated the interior of his restaurant.
The walls are covered with photographs of famous
comics and comedy album covers.

"This is like the Comedians' Hall of Fame," says
Uncle Frankie. "And we're gonna leave a space right
here in the middle for you, Jamie."

Uncle Frankie has even added some new
sandwiches to the diner's menu—all of them are
named for famous comedians. The Lucille Ball is a
meatball sub. The Jon Stewart comes with chunks
of stew beef and a schmear of cream cheese. The
Jerry Lewis? Lots of ham.

"Hollywood, here we come!" says Uncle Frankie
before we get down to practicing.

Did I mention that Uncle Frankie is flying out to
California with me?

And while he's out there, he'll still be my comedy
coach.

Not to mention my best friend in the whole
entire world.

Chapter 6

RINGING UP THE LAUGHS

The intense cramming continues as Uncle Frankie, once again, puts me in the hot spot—behind the cash register.

"Okay, folks," he announces. "There are only two and nineteen-thirty-sixths days left till the first round of the Planet's Funniest Kid Comic Contest finals. Everybody in line, pick a comic. Jamie? Ring 'em up and make 'em laugh."

I feel like a boxer working the speed bag. A football player running wind sprints. A guy playing croquet on horseback. No. Wait. That's polo.

"Rodney Dangerfield," says the first customer in line.

I tug at my collar, like Rodney would.

"What a dog I got. His favorite bone is in my

arm. I worked in a pet store and people kept asking how big I'd get."

KA-CHING! The cash register bell gives me a rim shot.

"Zach Galifianakis," says Mr. Cheeseburger with Fries.

"At what age do you think it's appropriate to tell a highway it's adopted?"

KA-CHING!

And so it goes—straight through the dinner rush.

Also in the line is one of my biggest fans, Mr. Burdzecki. He moved to America from Russia, so I always try to give him a classic Yakov Smirnoff joke.

"In America, you find where is Waldo," I say, putting on a Russian accent, so *Waldo* sounds like *Valdo*. "In Soviet Russia, Waldo finds where is YOU!"

Mr. Burdzecki cracks up and nearly laughs his furry hat off.

"Competition?" he says with a dismissive wave of his hand. "*Pah!* No contest. You funniest."

"I funniest?"

"*Da*. First you funny, then you funnier, now you funniest."

(I think they're studying comparatives and superlatives in his English as a Second Language class.)

When the dinner crunch is finally over, it's time for me to undertake the ultimate test of comedic endurance.

To push my training to the limit, I need to face

the toughest crowd any comedian has ever dared to perform in front of.

That's right. I'm heading home.

It's time to make the Smileys laugh (or at least smile).

Chapter 7

WANTED:
FUNNY BONES, FAMILY-SIZED

The Smileys, unfortunately, suffer from a rare genetic disorder called Idontgetit-itis.

Okay. I made that up. But I kind of wish it did exist so I could host a telethon to cure it. No matter how hard I try, I just can't make my aunt, uncle, and cousins laugh, chuckle, or giggle—even though I'm giving them surefire, can't-miss stuff straight out of the *Baby's First Jokes* joke book.

These people don't even titter. Come on—little birdies know how to titter.

The Smileys? There's not a tee-hee in the house.

But I keep plowing ahead. I move into some of my own school-based material.

"Today in the cafeteria, they served bean and bacon soup. I think an eighth grader got the bean."

Dead. Silence.

Mrs. Smiley raises her hand.

"Yes?" I say, hoping I'm not leaving flop-sweat stains all over her newly shampooed carpet.

"There was only one bean in the soup? That doesn't sound like a very good recipe, Jamie."

"Especially for a school," says Mr. Smiley. "You'd think they would have worked out a better bean-to-student ratio."

"Well," I say, "that's kind of the joke. See, the name of the soup is bean and bacon, so it sounds like there's only one bean. Tomorrow they're serving chicken noodle. I hope I get the noodle."

Silence.

Even deader.

Wait. In the front yard. Yes. A bird just tittered.

"There's only one noodle in their chicken noodle soup?" says Mrs. Smiley. "My goodness, Jamie, what on earth is wrong with the cooks in that cafeteria?"

Here's a hint for all you budding comics: Telling the same joke twice with a slight revision seldom makes it any funnier.

Ol' Smiler grumbles and slumps to the floor. I think he's trying to cover his ears with his paws.

But I keep going, even though I'm dribbling sweat like Dwyane Wade dribbles a basketball—hard and fast.

Mrs. Smiley raises her hand yet again.

"Yes?"

"I have an idea, Jamie," she says very politely.

"Great. What is it?"

"You should give us a signal. When you're actually telling a joke, raise one of your arms or wiggle your fingers."

I just nod.

And hope the judges out in Hollywood don't ask me to do the same thing.

Chapter 8

LAUGH, TWO, THREE, FOUR

Okay. All this cramming for the finals is making me feel like my head might explode and spew setups and punch lines all over the walls.

Because seven ate nine!

Swimming trunks!

It saw the salad dressing!

What do you get from a pampered cow?

What do lawyers wear to court?

Why is six afraid of seven?

Why did the tomato turn red?

Spoiled milk!

The Post office!

Law suits!

What do you get when you cross a fish with an elephant?

What starts with a "p" ends with an "E," and has a million letters in it?

I need a break—if only for ten minutes.

Plus, I sort of feel sorry for the Smileys.

They didn't ask to have their home invaded by me, a would-be comic in a wheelchair. Mrs. Smiley just happened to be my mom's baby sister. So, when Mom and Dad and my little sister, Jenny…

We'll skip that buzzkill. No need to bum us all out more than we're bummed out already.

Long story short, even though the Smileys don't laugh or smile, I've actually learned to love 'em. They're honest, hardworking, salt-of-the-earth-type people. Come to think of it, salt doesn't laugh much, either. Except maybe on movie popcorn. Especially if the movie is *Despicable Me*.

The Smileys were the first to lend a hand at the Good Eats by the Sea diner back when Uncle Frankie had a heart attack. Their older son, Stevie, actually pitched in and worked as a busboy, even though he would rather have been pitching me into a Dumpster.

Cousin Stevie Kosgrov and me? We have a few "issues." For instance, he's the middle school bully and I'm his favorite target.

That'll give you issues—not to mention a phobia

about being near him and a toilet at the same time. Stevie gives a world-class swirly whirly.

STEVIE KOSGROV
King of Swing

(He'll grab you by your ankles and swing you around until your pockets are empty.)

KOSGROV
THE
KRUSHER

LONG BEACH MIDDLE SCHOOL
ALL-PRO BULLY

STATS: #1 in Triple Nipple Cripples. 333 Atomic Wedgies Yanked. A Baker's Dozen of Hurtz Donuts.

FAVORITE SAYING: "I'm the Professor of Pain and my fists are gonna quiz your face!"

But Stevie isn't home.

So I decide to quit telling jokes and give the Smileys something they can all really use.

Laughing lessons. They're kind of like dance lessons for the face.

We'll start with our *ho ho ho*s and work up to the *ha ha ha*s. For beginner laughers, vowel consistency is crucial. Sure, with practice, you can mix up the

consonants and go with a *ba ha ha* or a *whoa ho ho*.
But jumbling up the vowels, like in *ha ho ha*, just
sounds weird—and kind of creepy.

I tell the Smileys to feel the laugh in their bellies
and let it ripple up to their lips. They look like they
ate a sausage sandwich too fast and have gas.

I have them stand on their heads and hold up a
mirror, just so they know what a smile is supposed
to look like—an upside-down frown.

Nothing works.

I just hope no Smiley ever lands a job as one
of Santa's helpers at the mall. Instead of *"Ho, ho,
ho!"* all that the kids will hear at the holidays is
"Harrumph, harrumph, harrumph."

Chapter 9

A NIGHTMARE BEFORE BEDTIME

I'm in my bedroom in the garage, flipping through my joke notebooks, trying to decide what's my best material for round one of the finals.

I mean—should I save the best of my best for round two so I finish big? Might be a good strategy. But if I do that, I run the risk of being eliminated in round one. In other words, if I save my best jokes for round two, I might be finished before I have a shot at making a big finish. I might wind up in Finnish finishing school finishing furniture.

Yes. I am still freaking out. The finals are now only 2.22 days away.

And then I nearly have a heart attack.

A monster bursts into my garage bedroom.

Is it a zombie? A vampire? A Teenage Mutant Ninja Turtle?

Nope. It's something much, much worse.

My cousin, the Master of Disaster, Stevie Kosgrov, dressed up in an early Halloween costume that chills me to the bone because it's a walking vision of my worst nightmare: Stevie as a stand-up comic.

It's just Stevie in a tuxedo T-shirt holding a flashlight and his little sister's hot-pink Hello Kitty microphone, but it's awful. And then he launches into his "act." Of course, since he's the number one bully at Long Beach Middle School, the only jokes Stevie knows are insults and put-downs.

"You know, Jamie, you're not as bad as people say. Nope. You're much, much worse. You're so ugly, Hello Kitty said good-bye to you. No, wait. Your face is very becoming. It's *becoming* uglier and uglier every time I see it."

My turn NOT to laugh or smile.

"What do you want, Stevie?"

"To save your butt."

"What?"

"You're a big-cheese comedian with lots of crazy fans, right? You ever hear about celebrity stalkers? The paparazzi? A kid in a wheelchair like you needs protection."

Stevie is making me so mad by reminding me that I'm "handicapped" I could spit nails—which, come to think of it, would be a very handy skill to have if you were a carpenter.

"I need protection?" I say, glaring at him hard.

"Yep, Crip. You need me." Stevie starts slowly pounding a fist into his open palm. Over and over and over. "I'm volunteering to be your bodyguard. OR ELSE!"

"Or else what? You'll beat me up?"

"Yep."

"So, basically, you would be my bodyguard, protecting me against...you?"

Finally, a Smiley smiles. "Yep. Because I've always wanted to visit Hollywood."

Chapter 10

KNOCK-KNOCK IT OFF

I may be sleeping, but the countdown clock keeps counting down.

So I keep cramming and practicing jokes—in my dreams.

It's like that Dickens book *A Christmas Carol*. While I'm asleep, I'm visited by the spirits of Comedy Past, Present, and Future. Unfortunately, none of these spirits bring their game-day material. All they seem to know are knock-knock jokes.

The Ghost of Comedy Past is extremely scary. He's this kid called Shecky from Schenectady, who

I met (and defeated) in the New York State round of the comedy competition. He's not any funnier in my dreams than he was onstage. Shecky steals most of his jokes from Henny Youngman and bad-pun websites. I think he stole his sense of comedic timing from a broken wristwatch.

"You wanna be crowned champ, take a tip from me: Steal from the best. It's what I do. That's why I'm doing my act in a wheelchair now, just like you. Wins me the audience's sympathy and guarantees me a parking spot near the front door. Ba-boom. Nailed it."

Chapter 11

LIVING THE DREAM— OR MAYBE THE NIGHTMARE

The next morning, there are only 1.75 days left until the finals.

I know this because the principal put it up on the reader board out in front of my school.

The second I hit the halls (with my new bodyguard, Stevie "Protection Racket" Kosgrov), even more girls are swooning over me—including Cool Girl, whose real name is Suzie Orolvsky, which is much harder to spell than Cool Girl.

True confession time: I have actually kissed Cool Girl, which, for an instant, turned me into Cool Kid. It was just that once. We almost kissed a second time—right before Gilda Gold kissed me. Then I kissed Gilda. I'm not exactly sure why. Sometimes it's confusing being a guy in middle school, especially if you're me.

Anyway, there are so many girls screaming and squealing at me on my last day in Long Beach before flying out to LA, I need my wingmen, Gaynor and Pierce, to help out with crowd control. They don't mind. Gaynor assures everybody he can do my signature even better than I can. "I can do the president of the United States, too. And that dude who signs all the money. I've got him down cold."

He also volunteers to handle any "kissing action" if, for any reason, I am unable to fulfill my duties as the most famous kid in Long Beach.

Jimmy Pierce, our resident genius, also helps

out. "I've designed and engineered a portable Jamie Grimm signature stamping machine. As an added bonus, my ink glows in the dark."

Pretty soon, we're all signing (and stamping) autographs like crazy.

I'm pretty sure Gilda—who maybe, kind of, sort of *might* be my girlfriend, due to the fact that she is the girl I kissed most recently—is cool with all this attention I'm getting from my adoring female fans.

Actually, I really haven't had much time to think about Gilda. I've been too busy cramming for the finals when I'm not autographing body parts.

Does that make me kind of a jerk? Probably. Because celebrity comes at a high cost. It's exhausting, grueling work. But, like they say, somebody's got to do it.

And Joey Gaynor's glad it's me.

So this is what heaven smells like. Strawberry lip gloss.

BEING GREAT CAN BE GRATING

Later, in class, Mrs. Kressin, the school's drama club adviser, gives us a very dramatic speech about "greatness."

(By the way, I think dramatic speeches are the only kind drama club advisers know how to give.)

"Remember the words of Sir Winston Churchill: 'The price of greatness is responsibility!' Or, as Albert Einstein so eloquently elucidated: 'Great spirits have always encountered violent opposition from mediocre minds.' In short, do as Judy Garland suggested...."

"Who?" I ask.

"Dorothy from *The Wizard of Oz*."

"Oh. Right. Her."

Mrs. Kressin raises a finger to boldly proclaim

the wisdom of Dorothy: "'Be a first-rate version of
yourself and not a second-rate version of someone
else.'"

Then she keeps going. I guess when you're a
drama teacher, you're used to memorizing long
speeches.

We were not put on this earth to be ordinary. Great men are like eagles, and not just because so many of them are bald. No. They dare to soar and build their nests on some lofty solitude. Or, in the words of the immortal Bartholomew J. Simpson, "Eat my shorts."

I have to wonder if Mrs. Kressin is talking to
me. But as inspirational as all her quotes are, I feel
more like a Woody Allen joke: "I've often said the

only thing standing between me and greatness is me."

Besides, I don't want to be great. I just want to be funny!

In exactly 1.5 days.

Chapter 13

READY! SET! NOT SO FAST...

The cramming once again continues after school at Uncle Frankie's diner.

"Last chance to rehearse, kiddo," he reminds me. "We fly to LA tomorrow."

I run down some one-liners about food. "Um, Jeff Foxworthy: 'You might be a redneck if you have a complete set of salad bowls and they all say *Cool Whip* on the side.' Paul Reiser: 'Get a good dog. We haven't picked up food in the kitchen in fifteen years.' Uh, Kermit the Frog: 'Time's fun when you're having flies.'"

"Good," says Uncle Frankie. "But remember, Jamie, you're always better when you make up your own material and give us your slant on life."

"I could cram some more on the plane," I say.

"No, wait. I can't. Airline seats are so tiny there isn't enough room to cram much except your knees up to your chin, which, in my case, is technically impossible."

Uncle Frankie laughs. "That's the stuff, kiddo."

"Okay. How about those overhead bins? You're supposed to stow your suitcase up there? How? They're so small, they can barely hold a lunch box. You ever been on a plane and heard people clap when it lands? Wasn't that the ending they were expecting?"

I'm about to launch into a whole bit about rolling my chair through airport security when my cell phone starts buzzing.

Then Uncle Frankie's starts buzzing, too.

Soon, push alert bings are popping up all over the diner.

Almost everybody in the restaurant simultaneously receives some sort of urgent message.

So we all check our phone screens.

NO.

THIS IS IMPOSSIBLE!

PUT ON THE BRAKES.

STOP THE JOKES.

KILL THE COUNTDOWN CLOCK. (Seriously. That thing is totally annoying.)

You ready for the big news flash?

The finals for the Planet's Funniest Kid Comic Contest have been postponed.

No joke—this isn't the big finish I was hoping for.

THE END OF THE WORLD (WELL, MINE, ANYWAY)

The news spreads like wildfire, which, I guess, means it destroys everything in its path—including all my hopes and dreams.

I'm not exactly sure what happened or why it happened.

I just know something has happened.

Something bad. No. Something HORRIBLE.

The finals will NOT be held in Hollywood anytime soon.

And there isn't any word about when (or if) they ever will be held.

The mysterious news is all over the Internet. Google's changed its logo and runs a banner headline on its news page.

IS THIS THE END OF COMEDY FOR KIDS AS WE KNOW IT? 🔍

Facebook posts are popping up everywhere.

Quick Facebook etiquette question—are you supposed to like something you agree with even if you don't, you know, *like* it?

Meanwhile, bloggers are blogging about it. Vine videos—six seconds of pure sorrow—are looping. Twits are tweeting the bad news.

 **LaffFan3000**
Right Now · 🌐

Hey, they canceled that kids' comedy show. Bummer. ☹ Anybody have a good recipe for buffalo wing tacos?

I feel like I'm Rudolph and somebody just canceled Christmas because of the fog. I'm never going to get my chance to shine.

Remember how I was such a big-shot celebrity this morning, signing all those autographs for throngs of adoring fans?

Funny how much can change in less than one day.

Actually, it's not funny. It's the opposite.

TV DINNER

I roll home to have dinner with the Smileys, so naturally that means the TV is on.

I guess this is how you have a family conversation around the dinner table when your family doesn't feel much like talking to each other. You let the TV do all the yammering for you.

Instead of Mrs. Smiley asking, "How was school today?" a commercial can ask, "Have you heard about the great new way to blast away blueberry stains?" Instead of getting caught up with everybody's day, you can keep up with the Kardashians and find out who they married this week.

Of course, if they run a movie trailer, it can make vegetables more exciting. Just change the words in your head: *"In a world where peas and carrots were never meant to be together on a plate, one boy was brave enough to attack them both with his fork."*

I could use this bit in my act. *If* I ever do my act again.

Hey, Smiley family, that pot roast looks good, but right now at Burger King you could be eating a Whopper with onion rings. And nobody would have to do the dishes.

Mrs. Smiley has the tabletop TV tuned to BNC and *The Evening News Tonight*.

By the way, how ancient are the people who watch the evening news, anyway? All the commercials are for prescription pills (with side effects that sound way worse than the diseases the pills are supposed to cure), adult diapers, and denture glue.

But tonight, in his wrap-up, anchorman Aiden Buchholz gives me some news I can actually use.

You gonna eat that, Jamie? I'm kind of hungry. They don't feed us inside this box except when a celebrity chef drops by the morning show.

"And finally," says Aiden Buchholz, "perhaps you've heard about the postponement of the Planet's Funniest Kid Comic Contest finals. Well, good news for the eight budding young comic hopefuls who were all set to fly to Hollywood. Don't worry. You will be appearing here, live on BNC, in exactly two weeks."

I nearly do a backflip out of my chair.

The finals were supposed to be on YUX, a basic cable channel.

Now they're going to be on BNC, one of the major networks?

This is unbelievable!

"Yes, it's true," says Aiden Buchholz, as if he read my thoughts. "BNC announced today that *we* will be broadcasting, live, the finals of the Planet's Funniest Kid Comic Contest."

He goes on to explain how eight of us will compete in a big live Elite Eight event, followed the next night by a results show. A couple of weeks later, the top four comedians will come back for the *final* finals and another live results show. The winners in both rounds will be chosen not by a panel of judges but by viewers' votes.

"America will decide who is the funniest kid on this particular planet." Aiden Buchholz gives the camera one of his sly looks. "Oh. One more thing. The prize has changed, too. Instead of one hundred thousand dollars, the top kid comic will take home one *million* dollars and be given the chance to star in his or her own sitcom on BNC!"

"Gosh," says Mrs. Smiley. "Two weeks. I guess that means you only have fourteen more days to prep your comedy routine, Jamie."

Yep. Start the new BNC TV countdown clock.

On second thought, how about we stop counting for a while?

Thanks.

Chapter 16

I'M BAAAAACK

The finals being moved to a major player like BNC (I think the letters stand for *Big Network Channel*) has made me even more of a celebrity at school.

The crowds that scattered away are now scattering back.

"Back off, people!" shouts Stevie. "In two weeks, my cousin could be a half-a-millionaire."

I gulp a little. "Half?"

"Yeah. You're giving the other half to me."

"Right. Forgot about that. Thanks a lot for reminding me."

"That's why I'm here, Jamie. To keep you humble. And terrified."

I don't have time to worry about Stevie shaking me down. I barely have time to go to class.

Everybody—from Mr. Sour Patch, the assistant principal, to dramatic Mrs. Kressin, to the guy who scrapes leftover chunks of cheesy nachos off our plates in the cafeteria—wants to have a picture taken with me.

Gaynor, Pierce, and Gilda want to hang out with me in the library like we used to during fifth period, but I can't do any of the stuff I used to do anymore.

With a million bucks and a TV show on the line, I can't waste too much time hanging out with them.

"I'm sorry," I say.

"Yeah," says Gaynor with a shrug. "You sort of are, dude. You suck the big radish."

I'm pretty sure we'll all be friends again as soon as this whole comedy contest is over. I hope so. But right now, I need to focus on THE FINALS.

The MILLION-DOLLARS-PLUS-MY-OWN-SITCOM finals!

TV OR NOT TV?

After school, I head to Uncle Frankie's diner for more cramming, but I don't get very far.

Long Beach is swarming with reporters from all the big-time entertainment and gossip TV shows. Stevie has granted them all "exclusive access" to me because he doesn't know what the word *exclusive* means.

First up is one of the reporters from *Extra DTVZ*, which, I think, stands for *Extra-Dumb TV Zoo*.

"Jamie," he says, "do you have a girlfriend?"

"Not really."

"What about this picture we took of you kissing a girl on the boardwalk last night?"

"Uh, sorry, that's not me."

"Our sources say it is."

"But the guy in the picture is standing. He's also bald."

The reporter nods earnestly. Cocks a questioning eyebrow. "Is that why you wear a wig, Jamie?"

"This is not a wig. It's my hair."

"It really is," explains Uncle Frankie. "Jamie's bringing back the whole 1970s John Denver look."

The reporter smiles some more and tries not to laugh.

People do that a lot when they check out my hair.

I chat with Biff Bilgewater from *Hollywood Tonight*. I think he uses Elmer's Glue to slick back his hair. He smiles so much, his teeth probably hurt. I know my eyeballs do. Talking to him is like staring into a lightbulb.

"Jamie, how does it feel to be rolling on up to the finals?"

I think he wants me to say something about my wheelchair, but I don't go there with him.

"Great, Biff. There'll be a lot of talented young comics on that stage with me."

"But, correct me if I'm wrong, you'll be the only comic working in a wheelchair. True?"

I try to make a joke out of it. "I think I might be the only one wearing a sweater vest, too."

Biff keeps smiling his cheesy smile at me. "Jamie, if you were a tree, what kind would you be?"

"Green, I guess. Except in the fall. Then I'd be kind of reddish orange."

Chapter 18

GOOD MORNING, AMERICA!

I am totally wiped out by the end of the day but say a quick prayer before my head hits the pillow: "Please, God—no more TV cameras. Until the finals, of course. You can't do live TV without TV cameras. But you probably knew that."

My prayer goes unanswered.

"Jamie?" Mrs. Smiley is at my door. She's in her bathrobe and curlers. I check out my alarm clock. She yawns.

Because it's 5:05 AM.

"There's a camera crew on the front porch."

"What?"

"They're from BNC."

Stevie comes up behind his mom. He's already in his bodyguard T-shirt and Ray-Ban sunglasses, even though the sun won't be up for an hour or so. "Want me to deal with 'em, Jamie? Toss 'em off the porch? Punch out their satellite dish?"

"No," I say, hauling myself across the mattress so I can transfer into my chair. "If they're from BNC, then this is probably part of the deal. Let's go see what they want."

"Jamie, my name is Hunter. I'm going to be your segment producer for the next two weeks."

"Um, okay. Why do I need a segment producer?"

"You ever watch *American Idol*? *America's Got Talent*? *America's Favorite Americans*?"

"I've seen the first two...."

"Right. Because the third one is my idea. Gonna be huge, kid, *huge*—once the network picks it up or listens to my pitch. But enough about me—this is about you."

"Okay."

"We need to make sure your backstory is super-sad and sappy."

"Really? Why?"

"Because that's what America wants, kid! Remember that country singer on *American Songster*, the girl whose father only let her order ketchup, mustard, and relish at McDonald's because ketchup, mustard, and relish are free and you can mix them in a cup of hot water to make McSoup?"

"Vaguely..."

"She went on to win the whole thing. How about the juggler on *Super-Talented Americans*? The guy who lost everything he owned when he rehearsed that bit with the flaming torches in his living room?"

"Kind of."

"You should. He went on the competition and now has his own show in Vegas.

"Why'd they both win? Because they gave us a chance to feel good about ourselves by feeling sorry for them."

"B-b-but—"

"Look, kid, for the next couple weeks, we're gonna follow you around town, school, your uncle's diner—wherever. We'll be shooting footage for your background piece."

"Okay."

"And, Jamie?"

"Yeah?"

"You wanna win this thing?"

"Sure."

"Then give me the schmaltz, kid."

"The what?"

"The mushy, gushy stuff." He gestures toward my wheelchair. "Make America cry, kid, and even if your act is lousy, I guarantee you'll roll out of Hollywood a winner!"

Chapter 19

SMILE—YOU'RE ON CANDID CAMERA, 24/7

The BNC crew follows me *everywhere*.

"America wants to see you brush your teeth, Jamie," says Hunter when I try to close the bathroom door for a little privacy.

"I'm, uh, going to do…other stuff, too."

"Really? Awesome. Hit your floodlight, Gunther," Hunter says to his camera operator. "America needs to see what really goes on in the handicap stall."

"No, they don't!" Somehow I slam the door shut.

It's the last shred of privacy I have all day. While I get dressed (which isn't as easy for me as it might be for you), they jump into my bedroom

"Does Jamie Grimm put his pants on one leg at a time?" booms Hunter. "Let's find out!"

When I wheel down the sidewalks of Long Beach, the camera crew walks backward in front of me.

"Just act natural," coaches Hunter.

You ever try to act natural with a camera, floodlights, and a microphone jammed in your face? I figure I need to do something funny to prove why I'm in the finals.

"Wow, you see that dog walking his person? If he's good, maybe the dog will give him a cookie shaped like a pizza. Hey, we give dogs cookies shaped like food *they* like."

My smile is so big and fake I know I look like a crazed jack-o'-lantern.

"Cute, kid," says Hunter. "But we don't need funny. We need to tug at America's heartstrings."

"All of them? That's a lot of strings. Like three hundred and fourteen million. And if they're heartstrings, they're gonna be kind of gross and—"

"Can the comedy, kid. Give me some schmaltz. Tell me what it's like knowing you'll never, ever walk down a sidewalk like a normal kid. Never jump rope or play hopscotch with all the other little children at school."

"I'm in middle school. Nobody hopscotches, not even the Scottish kids."

"Work with me, Jamie. You need to stir up the sympathy vote if you want to win, remember?"

"I don't mean to be difficult, Hunter, but I've never done that before. In fact, I've always done everything I could to *avoid* winning just because I'm in a wheelchair."

"Sure, kid. But in the early rounds, you weren't up against this kind of competition. You want to win? Make 'em weep. Tell 'em about life in the chair. How it feels to be an orphan. Show America how depressing it is for you to be *you* every day."

He's right. Some days it *is* hard being Jamie Grimm. Like today, for instance.

Chapter 20

GILDA TO THE RESCUE!

When we finally reach the driveway in front of Long Beach Middle School, all sorts of kids I don't even know are pushing and shoving each other, fighting to be on camera with me.

"I'm Jamie's best friend," says a kid I've never met. "Put me on TV!"

"I've known Jamie Flimm since kindergarten," says a girl who just last month told everybody my wheelchair smells like a gorilla's butt.

Fortunately, Gilda bursts out of the front doors.

"Jamie?" she hollers. "Wait right there!"

Her hair is even crazier and bouncier than usual as she races across the parking lot.

"Who's she?" asks Hunter.

"One of my real friends."

"Romantic?"

"Are you kidding? Gilda?"

Oh, crap. I realize I just basically dissed Gilda while the camera was rolling.

I try to backpedal, something that's extremely difficult to do when your legs don't work, by the way. "I mean, we're *friend* friends. We don't kiss, and junk. Well, we did. Once. But we're not going to do *that* again, that's for sure."

Now I slap my forehead. I'm still dissing Gilda.

"America loves a love story, Jamie," says Hunter as Gilda runs toward us. "Gunther? Zoom in. Jamie, kiss her!"

"What?"

"When the blond chick in the baseball cap gets here, kiss her, kid! And tell her to cry and show us all how hard it is to be in love with a crippled orphan!"

I'm about to explode.

Even though she's winded after her parking lot sprint, Gilda does my exploding for me.

"You want to lose a lens, camera jockey?" she sputters. "Stick it anywhere near my fist again and I'm shattering your glass."

"We're filming clips of Jamie's everyday life,"
Hunter tries to explain. "For his backstory."

"Not now, you're not," snaps Gilda, hands firmly
planted on hips. "Not if you think you're shooting
me. I didn't sign a waiver. You use one frame with
me in it, I'll sue. Did I mention my father is a
lawyer? He *loooooves* suing people."

"Gunther? Chantelle?" Hunter says to his team.
"Let's take five and let these two lovebirds have a
moment."

"We're not lovebirds!" I shout as the camera crew
walks away. "We're just friends."

Gilda's nose twitches a little when I say that.

Great. She ran to my rescue and I say thanks by hurting her feelings. You'd think, given my physical condition, I wouldn't jam my foot into my mouth on such a regular basis.

"I'm sorry, Gilda. I didn't mean to—"

She shakes her head. "Not important. This, on the other hand, is!"

She shows me her phone and the news flash she just found on the Web.

"You're going to be on *The Tonight Show* with Jimmy Fallon!"

"You're joking."

"Nope. Jokes are your department. I just bask in the reflected glow of your awesomeness."

Yes, she's busting my chops a little. But that's what friends are for: to remind you who you really are even when a major television network is trying to convince you to be somebody you're not.

"Did they say when I'll be on?" I ask, because I'm too nervous to scroll through the on-screen news alert myself.

"Yep," Gilda says with a slight grin.

"Well?"

"Uh, Jamie, why do you think they call it *The TONIGHT Show*?"

"I don't know. I guess because they already have *Today* in the morning and…"

Gilda's grin grows wider and I finally figure it out.

"Tonight? I'm going on Jimmy Fallon's show *tonight*?"

She tosses up both hands. "It's not the *Tomorrow* or the *Sometime Next Week* show, now is it, Jamie?"

Okay. Crank up a new countdown clock. I'll be on TV at 11:35 PM. Tonight.

"By the way," says Gilda, "Fallon tapes his show at five."

Oh-kay.

Chop six and a half hours off the clock.

Tonight is really this afternoon!

Chapter 21

UP PAST MY BEDTIME IN THE AFTERNOON

After school, we ditch Hunter and the camera crew for the ride into New York City and the *Tonight Show* taping.

"Sorry," Uncle Frankie tells the gang from BNC, "no room in the van. Stevie Kosgrov is a double-wide. Takes up two seats."

Uncle Frankie is taking me and cousin Stevie to 30 Rockefeller Center, the same building where, maybe a month ago, he took us to see *Saturday Night Live*. This time, I don't invite Gilda, Pierce, and Gaynor, even though they ask. That's three fewer people I have to face if I choke tonight.

I could tell they were a little hurt, but I have to do what's best for me, right?

Finally, some peace and quiet! Well, with Stevie here, I'll have to settle for quiet.

"I'm glad the camera crew isn't riding with us," I say, finally able to relax. They even wanted to come into the shower with me after gym class, where, by the way, I've developed a pretty good three-point

non-jump shot. (Not in the shower, in gym class!)
I may not be ready for murderball (wheelchair
rugby), but I might have a shot at playing
H-O-R-S-E in the driveway with my cousins someday.

"They're right behind us," reports Uncle Frankie.

I look back. They have their own van with a
satellite dish. They're probably shooting footage of
me with a zoom lens right now.

"You want me to make obscene gestures at them?"
asks Stevie, who's riding in back. "I could totally ruin
their footage." Stevie. Always a gentleman.

"No gesticulating, Stevie," says Uncle Frankie.

"Awww," Stevie moans.

"I mean it. Just because they're rude doesn't
mean we have to be crude."

"All right already."

Wow. Stevie Kosgrov actually listens to Uncle
Frankie. I told you the man was amazing, and not
just with a yo-yo and a burger.

Uncle Frankie glances over at me in the
passenger seat while he drives.

"So, Jamie, you ready for this? You know, for years,
a shot on *The Tonight Show* has been a lot of comics'
ticket to the big leagues. I'm talking 'unknowns' like

Jay Leno, David Letterman, Jerry Seinfeld, Eddie Murphy, Jim Carrey, Ellen DeGeneres—the list goes on and on. They were all nobodies until Johnny Carson gave them a chance to do their act in front of his curtain and a couple million eyeballs."

I can feel the sweat beading up on my brow. And in my armpits. Some droplets are trickling down my spine, too.

"Gross," Stevie groans in disgust. "You're gonna drown before we even get there."

"You'll do great, Jamie," says Uncle Frankie, my number one cheerleader. "You always do."

"Not really," I admit. "Remember—I have this bad habit of choking under pressure."

Stevie leans over the seat back and makes one of his crude gestures at me.

This one involves a balled-up fist.

"Not tonight, cuz. Otherwise, you can choke on this!"

So there you have it.

After I die on the most famous comedy stage of all time, Stevie Kosgrov will kill me again.

I have so much to live for.

HOLLYWOOD IN NEW YORK

I say good-bye to my family when we're upstairs at 30 Rock and I head backstage to the dressing rooms for Studio 6B—the same studio where Johnny Carson hosted *The Tonight Show* when *he* taped in New York City over forty years ago!

There's a lot of history in this studio.

And sweat. Most of *that* is coming from me.

Hunter and his camera crew have called it a night.

"We don't need to see you onstage," says Hunter. "We're more interested in your offstage life. Tomorrow, let's up our game a little, Jamie. Give me a story I can turn into a three-hankie tearjerker. *Ciao* for now!"

A nice production assistant named Stella Kim escorts me through the *Tonight Show* offices to my dressing room.

"We're having all eight finalists on the show over the next two weeks," she explains. "You live closest to New York City, so you're up first."

"Great," I say, my voice cracking on the *ate* part.

"We're going to park you in the greenroom for now. Oops. Bad choice of words."

"That's okay," I say.

"So how do you know Max Weasley?"

"Who?"

"Max Weasley. Biggest agent in all of Hollywood."

"Um, I don't think I know who he is."

"Really? He sure knows who you are. He's waiting for you in the greenroom."

She opens the door and I see this hyper guy in a shiny suit who is working two cell phones at once. He holds up a finger, asking me to give him a minute. Hey, it's only four-thirty. He can have a whole half hour.

He twirls both phones in the air and tucks them into his suit pockets like a gunslinger holstering a pair of six-shooters.

"You're Jamie Grimm, am I right?" Max Weasley says to me, kind of gesturing at my wheelchair.

"Yes, sir."

"How'd you like to be happy, Grimm?"

"Happy is good. Usually."

"I did some digging, Jamie baby. Can I call you Jamie baby, Jamie baby?"

"Actually, most people call me Jamie."

"Ah! But I'm not most people. I'm me. Max Weasley. Power agent to the stars. Brad. Matt. Sandra. SpongeBob. If you know 'em by their first names, I represent 'em."

He flicks me a business card.

"Jamie baby," he says, "you've got something."

"Oh, no, sir." I point to my legs. "This happened because of an accident, not a disease."

"Ha! Got it! You're funny, kid. A nonstop joke machine. Inside? I'm cracking up. Seriously."

"Thank you."

"Listen, lollipop, how'd you like to book a one-way ticket out to Hollywood for the big finals?"

"One-way? But how would I get home?"

"If we work together, you won't have to fly back to Nowheresville, Long Island. Hollywood will become your new home. Probably a mansion in Beverly Hills."

"Well, if I win and they put me in the sitcom pilot…"

"Forget sitcoms, kid. I'm talking movies. Summer blockbusters. I see you as the next big action hero."

"But, uh, I'm in a wheelchair," I say. "Most of my action involves rolling forward or tilting backward. I can also pop a pretty mean wheelie…."

"We'll shoot around the chair."

"Really? How?"

"Two little words: Green. Screen. This is the age of CGI, baby. With computers, we can do anything! Work with me and all your dreams will come true. I'll have you walking, running, jumping, and kicking bad guys off tall buildings in no time."

"Really?"

"Give me a green screen and some computer graphics and I'll have you flying to the moon!"

Wow.

I've never really wanted to fly to the moon, but the way Mr. Weasley says it, it sounds like it'd be the coolest thing in the world!

I'm brought back to earth by a knock on the door. It's the production assistant, Stella.

"You're on in twenty minutes, Jamie. Good luck."

"Thanks," I say.

I have a feeling I'm going to need more than luck to stop from bombing in front of Jimmy Fallon and the millions of people out in TV Land.

I'm going to need a few of those Hollywood green screen computer tricks.

Chapter 23

JAMIE AND JIMMY

There's a monitor backstage in the wings so I can watch the show while I'm waiting for my cue to go on.

Jimmy Fallon is chatting with his first guests, Taylor Swift and Daniel Radcliffe! Me? I'm sweating like a sumo wrestler wearing shrink-wrap in a sauna.

You sweat good, Grimm. You're so soaking wet, you could play one of the whales in _Free Willy 5!_

I'm about to bomb in front of Harry Potter and a singer with seven Grammy Awards. Maybe if I'm terrible, Daniel Radcliffe can cast a quick Obliviate spell to make everybody in America forget me while Taylor Swift sings her new hit single, "Jamie, We Are Never, Ever Appearing on the Same Show Together Again."

"Knock 'em dead, kid," Weasley says, "and you'll be living the dream out in Hollywood."

"And, uh, what happens if I don't do so good?"

"If you tank, this conversation never took place."

The audience starts applauding as a commercial break ends.

"All right," says Jimmy Fallon. "Coming out next, one of the eight kids who will be competing for the title of the Planet's Funniest Kid Comic over on BNC in a couple of weeks." He takes a beat. "Huh. Funniest Kid Comic. I always thought that was a contest for amusing goats."

Questlove, the drummer for Jimmy's house band, the Roots, gives that corny line a *badoom-boomp* rim shot on the side of his snare.

"Ladies and gentlemen," says Fallon, "put your hands together for the one and only Jamie Grimm!"

I roll out in front of the velvety blue curtain. To my right, in front of a New York City skyline backdrop, I see three silhouettes clapping for me: Jimmy Fallon, Taylor Swift, and Harry Potter.

Since this is a high-stress, nerve-racking, stomach-flipping situation, I do what I always do when I'm thrust into the spotlight.

I choke. And sweat. And forget my name.

But then Questlove gives me a drumroll and a cymbal crash.

BA-BOOM. It's like he found my On switch.

"Hi, folks," I say, waving from my wheelchair. "I know, I know. You look at me and you're shocked. You say, 'Oh, my. That poor, poor boy. It's just awful He's in…he's in…'"

I take a pause and add a dramatic "DUN-DUN-DUUUUN!"

Just when everybody in the audience thinks I'm going to say I'm in "a wheelchair," I hit them with my punch line:

"Middle school! Yep. I'm in middle school, folks. The worst years of my life. And trust me, I may be young, but I've already had some pretty rough years. When I was little, maybe two, I remember my parents used to make me watch…*Teletubbies*."

I wobble like a Weeble in my chair and gibber in my high-pitched Teletubbies voice, "Again! Again!"

The audience is howling.

I can hear Jimmy Fallon and his guests chuckling. That makes me feel way better. Because Harry Potter didn't need to use his Riddikulus spell to make everybody laugh.

I did it all by myself!

Chapter 24

LOOK AT ME!
I'M ON LATE-NIGHT TV!

The rest of my set is pretty good, too.

I end with a joke about the upcoming show on BNC.

"The Planet's Funniest Kid Comic. I wonder if other kids in the solar system are going to comedy contests on their planets. You laugh, but those Martians are very competitive. In fact, a Russian, an American, and a Martian were talking one day. The Russian said, 'We were the first in space!' The American said, 'We were the first on the moon!' The Martian just laughed. 'Big deal. We shall be the first on the sun!' The American and the Russian looked at each other and shook their heads. 'You can't land on the sun, you idiot,' said the Russian. 'You'll burn up.' The Martian laughed again. 'We're not stupid, Boris. We're going at night.' Thank you, folks. I'm Jamie Grimm."

The studio audience is clapping like crazy (yes, it helps that there are gigantic APPLAUSE signs flashing everywhere), and I roll over to join Jimmy at his desk.

That's right. I've made the big time.

Jimmy Fallon actually wants to talk to me!

Chapter 25

PREVIEW OF COMING DISTRACTIONS

Great set, Jamie!"

"Thank you, sir."

Jimmy Fallon gives me a look. Hey, I'm a kid and he's wearing a suit.

"You can call me Jimmy, Jamie," he says. "Or James, because that's, you know, the name on my birth certificate."

"Mine, too."

"So I could be a Jamie?" says Jimmy.

I nod. "And I could be Jimmy."

"So, we're, like, related?"

"I guess."

We're just goofing around, but the audience LOVES it. I get another round of applause.

"So the boys over at BNC are really torturing you kids, huh, Jamie?" Fallon says when we come back after another commercial break.

I play along. "How do you mean?"

"This long, drawn-out buildup to the big finish. First, eight of you compete in the semifinal finals. That's in two weeks, right?"

"Right."

"Then America votes and four comics go home. The four winners have to come back in, what, another two weeks for the *final* finals?"

"Yeah," I say with a smile. "I guess they wanted to give us time in between shows to catch up on our homework."

More laughs. Jimmy Fallon actually doubles over and claps a couple of times.

"You're good, Jamie."

"Thanks, Jimmy."

Fallon turns to his other guests. "Any advice for Jamie Grimm as he competes for one million dollars and his own sitcom? Daniel? You were a child star. What would you suggest?"

"Don't let them paint a scar on your forehead," says Daniel Radcliffe. "It took me a year to erase mine."

"Good tip. How about you, Taylor? You were about the same age as Jamie when you got your start in showbiz."

"Have fun," she says. "And never forget where you came from."

"Good advice. So, Jamie—where exactly do you come from?"

I'm sorry. I can't resist.

"Um, I forget."

And the audience cracks up.

All in all? *Tonight* is a very awesome night.

Click to see more

Chapter 26

HURRY UP AND WAIT

Jimmy Fallon was right. The waiting is the hardest part.

Day and night, I roll around Long Beach, cracking jokes to myself and anybody willing to listen. I remember what Shecky once told me about words with a *k* sound being funny. I try out a few on some pigeons I meet on the boardwalk.

Kiwi! Kazoo! Kaleidoscope! Kumquat! Cucumber! Pickle!

Funny places to live? Kankakee, Kalamazoo, Keokuk, and Cucamonga!

You think "k" words are funny? Try a pair with "P": Pigeon Poop, Puking Pig, Puzzled Pony.

The film crew that was documenting my every move in Long Beach has already flown back to Hollywood to splice together my "backstory" piece for the live TV show.

"We got all the footage we need, kid," the producer said after my wheelchair got stuck in a gutter during a downpour. There was a twelve-inch-deep pothole I couldn't see because of the miniature lake that had formed at the curb. Note to self—I need to check out wheelchair umbrella-holder options. Or buy a poncho.

Even though I kind of want to be, I'm never alone.

A big entourage follows me everywhere I go. And it's not my friends.

I haven't seen much of them lately. Between the new material I have to come up with and the reality show I was filming, I've had a hard time fitting them into my schedule.

This mob is a group of total strangers. See, after you've been on *The Tonight Show* and your routine goes viral on the Web, a lot of people you don't know all of a sudden think they know you.

I'm feeling big-time pressure to be funny 24/7.

So I spend my day spouting classic one-liners, one after the other in rapid-fire succession.

You ever see a boxer working a speed bag? Those leather balloons that keep snapping back every time you whack them? Well, instead of a punching bag, I'm banging out the punch lines, ones I've memorized from my very first joke books, just to keep my comedy muscles warm.

Gilda catches me joking to myself in the hall outside the boys' room.

"Jamie? You need to take a break."

"What do you know?" I snap at her.

"Whoa, ease up," says Gaynor.

"I agree," adds Pierce. "You're letting this competition get the best of you, Jamie."

"Well, that's what I need," I sort of yell. "My best! So butt out. All of you."

"Gladly," says Gilda.

And my three best friends in the whole world turn their backs and walk away.

I guess that happens to everybody once they become famous.

When I start telling knock-knock jokes to

random doors all over town, I realize even I can't take this anymore.

I raise both fists, Rocky-style, and shout at the sky, "Yo! Let's do this thing!"

I think an airplane up there heard me.

Because, finally, it's time for me and Uncle Frankie to fly to California for the big shoot-out at the comedy corral.

Chapter 27

FLYING TO THE LEFT COAST

Uncle Frankie and I have seats up front in the first-class cabin!

Yeah. When you do a TV show for a major network like BNC, they treat you like royalty, which I think some of the other people flying first class actually are. I hear someone being called Duke, although it could be the fluffy dog a few rows up.

I think the first-class flight attendants offer us pillows, warm mixed nuts, and free sodas.

They might even push a cart loaded down with three flavors of ice cream, hot fudge, butterscotch sauce, crushed walnuts, whipped cream, and candied cherries. Maybe they offer to make us our own anyway-you-want-it ice-cream sundaes.

I don't remember.

I spend the entire six-hour flight silently freaking out.

"Are you feeling okay?" asks one of the flight attendants. She's working her way up the aisle to offer everybody in first class some more free stuff. (I think this time it's gold-plated parachutes—just in case.) "You look as pale as a ghost."

I try to come up with a witty reply. Something like "I'm not pale. I'm just pigment challenged."

But all I come up with is "I'm a...uh..."

Uncle Frankie, who has the seat next to mine, chuckles.

"He's just nervous. Right, kiddo?"

"Uh..."

"Say," says the flight attendant, "aren't you that Jamie Grimm? You're one of those kid comedians. I saw you on *The Tonight Show*!"

"That's right," says Uncle Frankie, because he can tell from the look on my blank and ghostly-white face that I have completely forgotten how to form whole words, let alone sentences. "Of course, Jimmy Fallon asked *me* to be on his show, too."

"Really?" says the flight attendant, forgetting all about me and my ghostiness. "How come?"

"Two words. Yo. Yo. Do you mind?"

He shows her his Duncan Lime Light yo-yo. It changes colors while it spins.

"Had a heck of a time getting this past airport security," he jokes. "They thought it was a tiny flying saucer. I showed them the string and said, 'Don't worry. I keep my Martians on a short leash.'"

The flight attendant and the folks in first class who aren't in a total state of catatonic shock (that would be everybody except me) chuckle. Then, with the flight attendant's blessing, Uncle Frankie stands up in the aisle and puts on a show for the whole cabin.

The whole time Uncle Frankie is spinning and flicking and twirling his yo-yo, he keeps up a steady patter of funny one-liners. He starts pulling out all the stops and executing some of the more complicated moves—stuff like the Skyrocket.

"Hey, how do you get a baby astronaut to go to sleep? You rocket."

The Rattlesnake.

"So, did you hear about the snake that couldn't talk? Yeah, it had a frog in its throat."

People are laughing and clapping as he sets up his big finish—the Man on the Flying Trapeze.

"Hey, speaking of the circus, did you hear the bad news? Yeah. I feel sorry for my buddy, the human cannonball. He just got fired."

I think the entire plane would've given Uncle Frankie a standing ovation, except the pilot just turned on the FASTEN SEAT BELTS sign.

We've begun our initial descent into Los Angeles.

So I can head off to Hollywood and go make a fool of myself—*in front of millions of people!*

Chapter 28

THEY FUNNY, TOO

When you're in a wheelchair and need "a little extra time getting down the aisle," you're allowed to board the airplane before everybody else.

But you're going to be one of the last ones *off* the plane, too. That means our luggage is already waiting for us when Uncle Frankie and I reach the baggage carousel.

So are some very funny kids—my competition in the Planet's Funniest Kid Comic Contest—and they're flying into Los Angeles from all over the country, just like I did.

I see Ben Baccaro, the Italian Scallion, the kid comedian every girl in America is going to vote for.

Okay, they're going to vote for his tight T-shirt and muscles and that dimple in his chin. Ben is the Mid-Atlantic Regionals winner and hails from Philadelphia.

By the way, does anybody ever really use the word *hail* to say where a person is from anymore, or is the word *hail* exclusively reserved for bad-weather forecasts in the summer?

Yeah. My mind's still spinning. Never too late to work up some fresh material.

"Hey, Ben! How y'all doin'?"

That's Grafton Maddox Bacardi, the kid from Signal Mountain, Tennessee, who won the Southeast Regionals by mashing together his own material with recycled Larry the Cable Guy jokes.

Grafton Maddox Bacardi and Ben have
everybody at the baggage carousel doubled over
with laughter.

Including me.

Actually, I'm more or less doubled over with pain.
The kind that comes when you meet the two guys
you're going to lose a million dollars to.

Chapter 29

MEET CHATTY PATTY, DUMB AS A FOX

Uncle Frankie is yanking our bags off the conveyor belt when a very bubbly girl wearing a red-and-white-striped blouse skips up to where I'm sitting and waiting.

"Oh my goodness," she says in a thick Minnesota accent while she strikes a cutesy-pootsy pose. "You're dat Jamie Grimm, aren't you? You're dat cripple boy comedian."

She bats her eyes and smiles when she says "cripple boy," as if, somehow, that'll turn them into nice words.

"Jeepers, I am such a gul-dern big fan of yours, don'tcha know? I'm Chatty Patty. Actually, my real name is Patricia Dombrowski. My ancestors were unintelligent eyebrow pluckers who liked to glide down hills. How's by you?"

"Um, I'm fine. Long flight."

"I know. I just flew in from Minneapolis and, boy, are my arms tired. The flight attendants were very sweet, though. They said we could use our seat cushions for a flotation device. I'm going to take mine to the hotel swimming pool."

Chatty Patty, who lives in Moose Lake, Minnesota, does this sweet-as-pie but dumb-as-dirt act—sort of like a Midwestern version of Gracie Allen from the old *George Burns and Gracie Allen* radio show from way back in the 1930s.

Yes, I listened to every single Burns and Allen show on CD when I was recuperating in the rehab hospital.

I think Chatty Patty did, too. I recognize a lot of her one-liners from Gracie Allen's old routines.

Everybody in America thinks she's the sweetest, nicest kid in the whole wide world.

Me too.

Until she leans in, grabs hold of my armrests, and kind of sneers at me with breath that smells like sour bubble gum.

"For this whole competition you've had one joke, Jamie Grimm. Your wheelchair. Well, guess what, Wheelie McFeelie? Sure as God made dem little green apples, you're gonna lose dis thing. Big-time."

Chapter 30

SURF'S UP AND I'M DOWN

After my chat with Patty I'm pale as a ghost again.

"You ready to roll, kiddo?" asks Uncle Frankie, coming over with our bags.

"Yeah."

"You don't look so good. Was it something you ate?"

I nod. "Little green apples."

"When did you eat those?"

"In my most recent nightmare."

Just then, a camera crew bursts through the sliding exit doors, following a pair of bubbly young girls with shimmering hair.

It's Rebecca and Rachel Klein. Identical twins, they do this Valley Girl act as a comedy duo.

They're like a California version of Abbott and Costello, only blonder. Behind them are their younger brothers, Andrew and Alexander Klein. Rumor has it that Andy and Alex are already working on their "surfer dude duo" comedy act for *next year's* Planet's Funniest Kid Comic competition (if there is a next year).

"Everybody, look like you're long-lost friends," hollers the guy behind the camera, who I think is Hunter, the producer who came to Long Beach to film my "backstory" piece.

Chatty Patty is immediately "on."

"Golly, Becca and Rach," she gushes for the camera. "Thank you so, so much for dat roast beef recipe."

"Wha-huh?" says Rebecca, totally confused.

I, on the other hand, know exactly what Patty's talking about, because it's the setup for another Gracie Allen gag.

"That recipe you gave me," says Patty, winking at the camera. "You remember: 'Take one large roast of beef, one small roast of beef, and put them both in the oven. When the little one burns, the big one is done.'"

"Ooh," says Rachel. "That is so, like, grody and home ec-ish."

"Home ec is *sooooo* home '*yech*,'" adds Rebecca.

"Yo," says Ben, arching one of his eyebrows as he struts over to the two blondes (and the camera lens). "Are you two girls angels? Because you're definitely the answer to all my prayers."

"Lame, Ben," says Rachel.

"Rilly," adds Rebecca with an eye roll. Or it could have been Rachel who rolled her eyes and Rebecca who said Ben was lame. Like I said, they're identical twins, so it's hard to tell them apart.

Now Grafton Maddox Bacardi strides forward. "You know what my pappy used to say, ladies? Two can live as cheap as one, providin' one of y'all don't eat."

"Jamie?" whispers Uncle Frankie. "Shouldn't you say something funny? Everybody else is. This is probably for the TV show."

I raise my hand and wiggle my fingers at the Doublemint Valley Girls. "Uh..."

Yeah. I'm not even onstage and I'm already choking.

Fortunately, Uncle Frankie can tell I'm in no condition to be caught on tape. So he clears a path and we make it through the sliding glass doors and out to the sidewalk, where a whole bunch of limousines are lined up at the curb.

"Sirs?" A guy in a crisp black suit waves at us.

He's either our chauffeur or my funeral director, standing by for when I die onstage.

Chapter 31

I DON'T HAVE A GHOST OF A CHANCE

Hey there," Uncle Frankie says to the man in the dark suit. "I'm Frank Grimm. This is my nephew Jamie."

"Pleasure. I'm Charles. Your driver." He sounds like he could be somebody's butler.

"You got a lot of room in your vehicle," says Frankie, peering into the back of the stretch. "You want Jamie should carpool it with some of the other kids?" he asks the driver.

"No need. Each contestant has been provided with his or her own private limousine."

"Kind of a waste of gas, don't you think?"

The driver points toward the open door. "I am not

paid to think. Do you require assistance with your wheelchair?"

I shake my head.

"We got this," says Uncle Frankie.

We quickly do our standard transfer from the chair into the car—even though I have to sling my butt sideways with a little more oomph than usual to make a soft landing on the limo's very low bench seat.

Uncle Frankie folds up my chair, stows it in the trunk, and climbs in the back with me, and we hit the highway.

In Los Angeles that means we basically do two, maybe three, miles an hour in bumper-to-bumper, smog-choked traffic on a six-lane strip of hot concrete.

The back of the limo feels like a sauna. I'm sweating so much, my shirt feels like I went swimming in it.

Then, all of a sudden, I'm freezing. My teeth start chattering. Now I feel like somebody dumped a bucket of ice cubes down my pants.

"You okay, kiddo?" asks Uncle Frankie. "You don't have to do this if you don't want to, you know."

Yes, I do, I think. *Everybody is counting on me. I'm Jamie Grimm. The sit-down comedian. I funny.*

"I'll be okay," I say. "I guess I just need a Coke or something to settle my stomach."

Uncle Frankie finds one for me in the limo's refrigerator. "Here you go, kiddo. And, Jamie?"

"Yeah?"

"Stay away from those little green apples."

Chapter 32

ONE DAY I SPENT
A WEEK IN LA TRAFFIC

The limo crawls up the 405 Freeway for what seems like forever.

It takes us an hour to drive five miles.

"Welcome to LA," says Uncle Frankie. "Reminds me of that Conan O'Brien joke: 'In Russia, there was a one-hundred-and-twenty-five-mile traffic jam that had drivers stuck in traffic for over three days. Here in Los Angeles, that's known as Friday.'"

I laugh. The driver laughs.

After his yo-yo show on the plane and his quick monologue in the back of the limo, I'm thinking Uncle Frankie should put on a bowl-cut hairdo wig, borrow my wheelchair, and take my place in the finals.

Eventually, the limousine escapes the freeway and takes us to the Four Seasons Hotel in Beverly Hills.

"All the contestants will be staying here," says the driver as we pull up a very fancy driveway to the hotel's even fancier entrance.

About six guys in uniforms and gloves and snappy hats start opening doors and grabbing our luggage and unfolding my chair and saying stuff like "Welcome back, sirs," even though Uncle Frankie and I have never been to this swanky hotel before.

"We're here for the kids' comedy show," says
Uncle Frankie, slipping the head bellhop a wrinkled
one-dollar bill. "We just need to find our room and
freshen up."

"Hey, Jamie!"

I look toward the lobby. It's her.

Judy Nazemetz. The kid version of Tina Fey. The
one comic who's actually been kind to me on several
different occasions throughout all the rounds of this
competition.

"Can I go say hi to Judy?" I ask Uncle Frankie.

"Sure, kiddo. I'll check us in and have the bags sent up to the room. I'll leave you your key at the front desk."

"Thanks."

Uncle Frankie checks his watch. "We need to head to the studio in three hours. Whaddya think, Jamie? Do I have time for one of those honey-and-papaya facials?"

"Seriously?"

"Well, I am kind of hungry."

"You're joking. Right?"

"Of course I am, kiddo. We came out here to make people laugh, remember?"

Right.

Somehow, I keep forgetting that.

Chapter 33

JUDY, JUDY, JUDY!

Smiling, I roll over to say hi to Judy Nazemetz.

I beat Judy in the New York State round of the competition, but she became the judge's wild card choice for the Northeast Regionals, where she came in second and earned a trip to the semifinals in Las Vegas. The comic who beat her at the regionals in Boston? That would be me.

"Hey," I say when I roll into the sparkling marble lobby to greet her.

"Hey. Welcome to Hollywood. This your first trip to LA?"

"Yeah. Love what they've done with the freeways."

"Oh," says Judy, with a twinkle in her eye, "you enjoy spending time in slow-moving parking lots?"

"Oh, yeah. I could spend a whole week on the LA freeway."

"You will," says Judy, picking up on my riff. "In one afternoon."

"And when the smog lifts in Los Angeles…"

"UCLA."

We laugh, even though that "you see LA" joke is corny enough to get us both kicked out of the finals. We keep riffing off each other.

What can I say? Judy is nice. It's great to see her again.

"I hope you win, Jamie," she says.

"Really? Because I sort of hope *you* do."

"Well, in this round, there are going to be four winners, correct?"

"Yeah," I say, realizing she's right. "Guess we both have a fifty-fifty shot at moving on, huh?"

"Yep."

Then my personal smog disappears. All of a sudden, I'm filled with nothing but golden California sunshine and Hollywood hope.

Because—don't tell Gilda—Judy Nazemetz leans down and kisses me.

This isn't really a kiss. It's more research for that joke about braces.

Watch your back, Jamie.

Chapter 34

SHOWTIME!

The first of the two finals shows goes on the air, live, at eight o'clock Eastern time.

That means five o'clock LA time.

So, after a quick lunch and an even quicker change of clothes, we climb back into our stretch limo for the one-hour drive to the BNC studios, which are, maybe, three miles from the hotel.

We could've walked it faster.

Yes. Even me. *I* could've walked it faster.

When we get to the Planet's Funniest Kid Comic Contest set, I see four of my comedy idols.

Ray Romano is, once again, the host of the show. The judges will be Louis C.K., Tina Fey, and Eddie Murphy. That's right. *The* Eddie Murphy. The funnyman who did the voice of Donkey in all the *Shrek* movies. He'll be here to see me make a jackass of myself.

Of course the judges don't really get to judge us. Well, they do, but it doesn't count. They'll critique our performances and say stuff like "You stink, Jamie, but it's up to America to decide if you smell worse than a hard-boiled egg that's been soaking in a pickle juice jar for six months," just like the judges do for the finals of *American Idol* and *America's Got Talent*.

Two seconds after we arrive (well, that's how it feels), the show goes on the air.

Live!

Chapter 35

STIFF COMPETITION
(I'M THE STIFF)

Contestant one, Chatty Patty Dombrowski,
heads to center stage.

She's wearing a matchy-matchy outfit that's
so red-white-and-blue it makes her look like a
sideways flag.

"Golly, America! I'm so gul-dern glad to be here,
don'tcha know? I hail from Minnesota, which is a
weird word. Not *Minnesota*, which I guess *is* weird. I
think *Minnie-sota* is Indian for 'small Coke.' No, I was
thinkin' about dat other word. *Hail.* Isn't dat the stuff
that falls from da sky during a gul-dern tornado?"

Wow. I was going to make a very similar *hail*
joke. Guess I better cut it.

I have to admit, the seven other comics in the Elite Eight, even Chatty Patty, are a pretty funny bunch. Guess they wouldn't've made it this far if they weren't extremely talented.

Just like on *Idol* or *AGT*, when a comic wraps up a set and listens to the judges' comments, the contestant makes some kind of goofy hand gesture to remind viewers what number to vote for with their texts and phone calls.

Chatty Patty has a big purple foam finger so she can show us she's "number one" (and a Vikings fan).

Next up is Grafton Maddox Bacardi.

When number three, Ben Baccaro, takes the stage, the girls in the studio audience start screaming and squealing so loudly that One Direction would be jealous.

I'm pretty sure Ben just won half of the vote. Maybe more.

But the audience screams even louder when the fourth contestant, Judy Nazemetz, hits the stage. After all, Judy's a TV star. She's also extremely hysterical and has this relaxed way of telling a crazy, convoluted story filled with wacky characters with even wackier voices.

If you ask me, Judy is the funniest kid comic on the planet.

But there are four more comics to go in the second half of the show, including yours truly.

I'll be the last one up.

You know that old saying "They saved the best for last"? Well, whoever said it wasn't talking about this show.

I'm going to bomb.

Unless I choke.

Or die.

Maybe all three.

COUNTING DOWN THE COMICS

Antony Guerrero, the Southwest Regionals winner from Albuquerque, New Mexico, is the fifth comic to step up to the microphone.

Sorry I'm a little late. Before they'd let me on stage, they needed to check my papers. I told them my ancestors have lived in New Mexico so long that the first Guerreros just called it Mexico. Because that's what it was.

Guerrero is extremely hip and edgy. Does a whole bit about the Pilgrims being the original "illegal immigrants."

"They were basically boat people with funny hats," he says. "And none of them could speak the language. The Native Americans, the ones who had all the food that first winter, couldn't understand a word these illegals were saying. The Pilgrims were all 'good morrow' and 'prithee' and the locals, like Squanto, the real Americans, they were like, 'Hey, Buckle Hat. You come to this country, learn how to speak Pawtuxet, for crying out loud! And why do you keep stuffing bread crumbs up inside that turkey? Bread crumbs are for the birds. And, puh-leeze, will you people please quit carving faces into all the pumpkins? Seriously. I prithee.'"

He's pushing the edge of the envelope. Refusing to be politically correct.

Which, come to think of it, is something I used to do.

The sixth comic, representing the Mountain States, is a fat, almost bald, schlumpy eleven-year-old who looks a lot like the famous fat, bald, schlumpy adult comedian Louis C.K., one of our

judges. The kid even wears a sloppy, food-stained
sweatshirt. His name is Samuel Bromley Oravetz.
It takes Ray Romano about three minutes to
pronounce all that.

Second to last, we have the Klein sisters, Rebecca
and Rachel. They do a very funny back-and-forth
bit that reminds me of the Marx Brothers' classic
"Why a Duck" routine.

When they're done, Rebecca holds up five fingers, and Rachel holds up two. "Because," says Rebecca, "five plus two is fifty-two!"

"Uh, hello? Earth to Rebecca. It's not fifty-two. It's twenty-five."

"*What*-ever."

Next up, number eight, is me.

My heart is in my throat, which, if you check out a biology book, is a very bad location for it.

Ray Romano does my intro.

I roll onstage.

I can't remember a single joke. Just a line from every gladiator movie ever made: *We who are about to die salute you!*

Chapter 37

WAS I EVEN ON THE SHOW?

I'm pretty sure I bombed.

Yes, now I not only forget my jokes, I also forget how I did when I told them. *If* I told them. My mind is a blank. My performance? A gaping black hole from which nothing funny could possibly escape.

This will be my last show in the competition. I'm sure of it.

Compared to the sensational seven who went up to the microphone before me, I am, definitely, the planet's most forgettable kid comic.

You know that fifty-fifty chance Judy and I had of moving on to the next round? She still has it. Me? I'm feeling fifty-fifty the other way.

But I won't know how bad I was for sure until tomorrow.

The results show, or, as I'm calling it, *Bye Bye Jamie.*

The rest of the pages in this book? I guess those are filled with pictures of me being a loser.

In a wheelchair.

I'll always have the wheelchair.

Chapter 38

AND THE LOSERS ARE...

I don't eat or sleep or do much of anything for twenty-four hours.

Then the eight of us troop back to the same studio for the results show. Millions of texts and phone calls and online votes have been tabulated. All we have to do is endure one very long, drawn-out hour until Ray Romano, at the last possible moment, tells America who is moving on to the finals and who is heading home.

Sweat is dribbling down my brow and my back.

"Eight comedians performed," says Romano, "but only four will move on to the finals. That means..." He takes a big, dramatic pause. "Four kid comics are going home to do homework and wash dishes and mow the lawn and do all the stuff kids are supposed to do but mine never do."

Then he asks the judges what they think of all of us. They tell some jokes.

Then they show some clips.

Then they tell some more jokes. Special guest star Jeff Foxworthy comes on and tells some jokes, too.

The suspense is killing me. Literally. I think I just aged, like, twenty years in ten minutes. And my heart has migrated up to behind my eyeballs.

I work on my non-victory speech in my head.

"I'm sorry I lost, Long Beach. I'm sorry I lost, Uncle Frankie. I'm sorry I lost, Uncle and Aunt Smiley." Then I get a lump in my throat wondering if there's a TV up in heaven. *"I'm sorry I lost, Mom and Dad. I'm sorry, Jenny. At least you three didn't have to be here to see me lose."*

"Judy Nazemetz and Ben Baccaro, please step forward."

Finally. Ray Romano has the results envelopes in his hands. He tears open the first one.

"Judy. You are…"

Big pause.

"…going…"

Bigger pause.

After Ray Romano stretches it out longer than a hot strand of chewing gum stuck to your shoe in the summer, he finally fills in the blanks:

"...to the finals!" The crowd goes wild. Cocky Ben winks because he figures he's moving on, too.

He isn't.

"Sorry, Ben," says Ray. "You're going home."

Chapter 39

AMERICA HAS SPOKEN!

The eliminations continue.

Grafton Maddox Bacardi and Antony Guerrero are told to step forward next.

Grafton Maddox Bacardi is going home. Antony, the edgy comic, is safe.

Next up to the chopping block, it's the Klein sisters and Chatty Patty.

The Valley Girls are heading back to the Valley.

Patty is moving on.

"Samuel Bromley Oravetz?" says Ray Romano. "Please step forward. All three of you."

Oravetz slumps into the spotlight and scratches the seat of his pants with one hand, his belly button with the other.

"Jamie Grimm? Please, uh, *roll* forward."

I do as instructed. In my head, I'm still apologizing to everybody who was counting on me to win this thing.

Ray Romano tears open the envelope with his finger. In slow motion.

He sloooowly pulls the card out.

He takes for-ev-er to read what is written on it. My whole world has turned into the Los Angeles freeway system. Nothing is moving. I'm going nowhere.

Except back to Long Beach.

"Samuel Bromley Oravetz?" says Romano in super-slo-mo. "You...are...going..."

My heart stops beating. I close my eyes.

"…home."

My eyes pop open. I blink a couple of times.

"Jamie Grimm?" says Ray Romano. "You're our final finalist! Congratulations!"

Somewhere off in the distance, I hear Uncle Frankie's ear-piercing whistle. "Way to go, kiddo!" he shouts. "You won!"

Judy Nazemetz runs over to my chair and throws her arms around me and kisses me—right on the lips.

On network TV.

I turn red. And smile for the first time in days.

Now Chatty Patty and Antony Guerrero come over to join us. Apparently, we're the four finalists in the Planet's Funniest Kid Comic Contest.

I guess I did pretty good.

I guess I'm one of the four funniest kids on the whole entire planet!

"Congratulations," I hear Judy whisper under all the audience applause. "We both live to bomb another day."

That makes my grin grow even wider.

We fist-bump on it.

"Sympathy vote," Chatty Patty says through her fake smile.

But I don't care. I don't have to give my "I'm sorry I lost" speech. At least not for a few more weeks.

America voted, and I am definitely, officially, certifiably funny!

Not that I'm going to get a big head about it or anything...

Chapter 40

A HEAD TOO BIG FOR MY HAT

Yes, I head home to Long Beach the same humble and modest Jamie Grimm I was when I left.

Who needs an airplane to fly home? I'm my very own hot-air balloon!

WE ♡ JAMIE!

Okay. Maybe I'm just a little puffed up about winning.

But I'm told your head always swells a little when you fly all the way across the country. And the truth is, I'm even bigger than I was before.

In fact, I'm the biggest hero in this Long Island town since Billy Crystal.

That's right, another one of the planet's funniest comedians grew up in Long Beach on Long Island. Billy Crystal—the star of *Saturday Night Live*, *When Harry Met Sally...*, *City Slickers*, *The Princess Bride*, and, most impressively, the voice of Mike Wazowski in *Monsters, Inc.* and *Monsters University*—used to hang out in all the places where I hang out now.

I'm thinking there's something magical in this little seaside paradise that, every generation or so, makes one kid in Long Beach really, really funny.

At least that's what I'm telling everybody.

What I'm pretending to believe.

At school, I am one of the cool kids. Okay, I am the Coolest Kid. Ever.

Hey, I've been on national TV. I won a contest. Billy Crystal probably wants me to do a voice in the next *Monsters* movie. What could be cooler than that?

Life is great. No, my life is awesome.

There is only one teensy-weensy, tiny problem.

Before I went on, before I did whatever jokes I did (and can't remember), BNC ran that sappy background piece the camera crew filmed about me in Long Beach.

As Smokey Robinson's song goes: Now there's some sad things known to man/ But ain't too much sadder than the tears of a clown/When there's no no one around...

TEXT TO VOTE JAMIE GRIMM PLANET'S MOST PATHETIC KID

All of America got to see me stuck in the gutter. They watched me flip through an old family photo album and sob (I couldn't help it) over pictures of my mom and dad and little sister, Jenny. They saw me wrestle with denim as I wiggled around on my bed, trying to pull on a pair of jeans over my dead legs.

Then there were the grainy newspaper headlines and slow-motion *Action News* footage of swirling emergency lights from the car crash that left me an orphan. After that came some dramatic still shots of me struggling through physical therapy at the rehab hospital.

Yeah.

Chatty Patty was right. America gave me their pity vote. That's how I survived the first round of eliminations.

But don't worry.

I can still fool people into believing I'm the kid who WON the big contest because I'm incredibly funny and extremely talented.

What other choice do I have?

Go all honest and admit that I'm the biggest loser ever?

Because that's the real truth.

Chapter 41

WITH FRIENDS LIKE THESE...

At school, when my "friends" Gaynor and Pierce back me into a corner near our lockers, I go ahead and let them lecture me.

Dude, something bad happened to you out in Los Angeles.

Did a snake bite your head?

When they're finally done giving me a piece of their minds, I rank on them in return.

"You know what I think, guys? I think you two are jealous. You wish you could be famous like me, but you never, ever will be. You know what else I think? I think I'm kind of ashamed and embarrassed for you both. Seriously. Jealousy and envy are such a waste of time."

Pierce and Gaynor drop their jaws like they can't believe what I'm saying.

Neither can I.

And to make matters worse, Gilda comes over and it's obvious she heard it all. "We're your friends, Jamie," she says, trying to make peace.

If they were truly my friends, they would know how I really feel, right? So instead of explaining something I don't want to explain, I flip out.

"No, you're not. You just want to glom on to my fame and bask in my glory. Face it, that's all you guys have ever wanted!"

Chapter 42

TONIGHT'S SPECIAL: ANOTHER LECTURE

I get yet another lecture from Uncle Frankie that night at the diner.

What'd you do, Jamie? Hook your mouth up to a bicycle pump?

"I'm just being honest here, Jamie. I gotta agree with your friends. You've got a bad case of swollen-ego-itis complicated by severe stuck-upness."

"Those guys are not my friends. They're just a bunch of fame moochers."

Yes, when I become a jerk, I go all in.

Uncle Frankie shakes his head. "Those three were your pals long before you even entered your first comedy contest."

"A contest I only entered because *you* made me do it!"

Yeah, I'm kind of lashing out at everybody I love because I know the truth: I'm a loser who only made it into the Final Four because I rolled onstage in my wheelchair.

I'm one of those YouTube clips that get passed around a billion times—not because my act is funny. Because I'm so pathetically sad and it makes people feel better about themselves to cheer me on.

"You pushed me onto that stage, Uncle Frankie, and only because you wanted to relive your bygone glory days as a yo-yo champion."

Uncle Frankie cocks an eyebrow. "Seriously? That's what you think?"

"Think? That's what I know."

Uncle Frankie sighs. "You've changed, Jamie. And not for the better."

"I know. I used to be able to walk."

"This isn't about your legs, Jamie. It's your head that's got me worried."

"You mean me thinking I'm a super-important comedian?"

"Yeah."

"Well, stop worrying. It's just an act. I'm just pretending to be a big shot."

"What? Why?"

I take a deep breath. "So people will hate me so much for being a conceited twit, they won't have time to realize I'm not funny."

"You? Not funny?"

"Come on. I only made it to the Final Four because I'm the sad little crippled kid. I won America's sympathy. Me thinking I could actually win a comedy contest? That's the biggest joke I've ever heard."

Chapter 43

WE INTERRUPT THIS MELTDOWN FOR A VERY IMPORTANT ANNOUNCEMENT

Yep, we have another delay of game.

This time, it isn't the countdown clock or a television network's fault.

In fact, this time, it has absolutely nothing to do with the Planet's Funniest Kid Comic Contest or the Smileys or Chatty Patty or Gilda Gold or even me. This time, it's something way more important than the most important thing in my life.

Something way more dangerous, too.

Before Uncle Frankie can give me the old spiel about how I'm not a loser, blah blah, the *Seinfeld* rerun on the TV cuts out and is replaced by an intense STORM ALERT graphic. If letters could talk, these would be screaming bloody murder.

"This just in from our weather center," says an even more intense voice. Now the TV screen behind the counter is filled with satellite footage showing a swirl of angry white clouds whipping around the eye of the storm. The cloud whirl looks like it covers the entire Atlantic Ocean.

"The hurricane we've been tracking all week has unexpectedly changed course!" shouts a weather guy who's wearing a yellow rain slicker and standing on a beach in the howling wind.

Why do they do that? Why do TV people think they need to stand in knee-deep water and hang on to trees, lampposts, and their baseball hats to tell us about a storm?

This particular weather guy looks like the fisherman on the fish sticks box, except he's about to be blown sideways.

"Revised estimates," the reporter yells over the roar of the wind and the crash of the waves, "show Hurricane Sam making landfall somewhere along the Long Island coast in the next few hours! We can expect quite a storm surge. Flood warnings are in effect for the entire region...."

"Maybe it'll miss us," I say.

Then again, maybe it won't.

Because the next graphic on the TV screen shows the storm making a beeline not just for Long Island.

It's heading straight for Long Beach.

Chapter 44

SAM I AM. BAM!

That night, Hurricane Sam slams into Long Beach. At high tide. Under a full moon.

No wonder the TV is calling Hurricane Sam the storm of the century.

It's scary.

No joke.

Because the storm wasn't originally supposed to blow this way, Long Beach didn't really prepare well enough. The Smileys and I huddle in the living room all night as the wind shakes the walls and roof like the wolf in "The Three Little Pigs." The power goes out and seawater starts seeping into the house. We had no idea it was going to be this bad.

The next day, I venture out to see the damage.

I'm blown away.

The whole boardwalk is demolished. Frankie's Good Eats by the Sea is wrecked. The fish and seafood in Uncle Frankie's freezer got to meet some of their long-lost cousins when the Atlantic Ocean rolled through the front windows for an unannounced visit.

My home, Smileyville, is totally flooded with two feet of water and sludge. It's deeper in my bedroom because the garage sits lower than the rest of the house. All my comedy notebooks and funny DVDs and jokelopedias are floating around like the flotsam and jetsam bobbing belowdecks in that movie *Titanic*.

Worse than anything that happened to me on national TV. In fact, seeing all this destruction—how quickly homes and businesses and whole lives can be swept away—makes me realize that my problems are nothing compared to what just happened to my neighbors.

I'm reminded of something I heard once: If we all took our problems and threw them into a pile next to other people's and saw what *they* had to deal with, we'd grab our own problems back as fast as we could.

So what if I only moved up in the comedy contest because of the sympathy vote?

Uncle Frankie just lost his diner, his whole life.

Hurricane Sam is like a wake-up call: a bucket of cold water tossed in my face.

Except this cold water is also salty. And full of fish.

Chapter 45

MOVING TO COT CITY

With most of Smileyville swimming in seawater, it's basically uninhabitable. We're ordered to evacuate the house.

Cousin Stevie refuses to leave without his most prized possession. So he slogs through the ankle-high water to his bedroom and grabs his money box. It's where he keeps all the cash he collects shaking kids down outside the cafeteria.

"It means more to me than anything in the world! Even my monogrammed set of brass knuckles."

Four burly National Guardsmen hoist me up and load me into the back of their army truck. We power our way through the flooded streets and make it to the high school, where the Red Cross has set up an emergency shelter inside the gym.

I see some of our neighbors. Ol' Smiler wags his
tail when he sniffs a few familiar butts.

And then I see the Golds. Gilda's family.

She is there, too, of course.

It's time to face the music.

She goes first. "Hello, Jamie. You guys okay?"

"Yeah. I guess. The house is a mess...."

"Ours, too."

"I always wanted an aquarium in my room," I joke, "but this is ridiculous."

Gilda grins.

"Sorry," I say. "I…"

"Yeah. I know. Me too."

She leans down and, even though our clothes are like wet, squishy sponges, we hug. It's probably the best hug I've had in months.

Chapter 46

PLAYING THE RED CROSS ROOM

Hey, you're Jamie Grimm!" says this little kid on a nearby cot. "I saw you on TV!"

I kind of smile and wave.

"You're that comedian kid, am I right?" says a guy sipping coffee out of a paper cup.

"He's funny," says somebody else. "Do that politically incorrect bit you did on TV."

"And that jingle you made up. You know, that funny car commercial you sang on the show. That was hilarious."

Wow. These people remember more of my Hollywood performance than I do.

"Thanks, you guys," I say. "Maybe some other time, okay?"

"What?" says the guy with the coffee. "You got

some previous engagement or something tonight?"

"No, but, well…I'm not sure this is the right time and place for, you know, comedy."

"How come?"

"Well, sir, a lot of these people don't have much to laugh about tonight."

"I know," he says. "That's why they need you to give 'em a smile."

"He's right, Jamie," whispers Gilda. "Everybody in Long Beach could use a good laugh tonight."

"Seriously?"

She nods. "It's what non-jerk Jamie would do."

"Yeah," I say. "I remember him."

I roll forward a couple of feet. Find an open spot in the sea of cots.

There's no microphone. No spotlight. No Ray Romano giving me a big introduction.

I just take a deep breath and start, trusting that Gilda (who has the best and bubbliest laugh in the world) at least will chuckle, even if nobody else finds me particularly funny on this gloomy night.

"Um, hi, everybody. I'm Jamie Grimm. I'm also soaking wet, but, hey, tonight, who isn't?"

Gilda giggles. I keep going.

Okay, if I've ever been funny, **PLEASE** let me be funny now! And sorry about everybody calling Hurricane Sam "an act of God." I figure it really wasn't your idea.

"So, anybody here ever gonna name a kid Sam? Didn't think so."

I hear some muted laughs.

"How come they give hurricanes and storms such ho-hum, boring names? Sam. Kate. Barry. Sounds like those kids who used to be on *The Brady Bunch*. They should give hurricanes names like Shamu. Or Bertha. 'Look out. Here comes Big Bertha!' Or Conan. That'd be a good name for a storm. Not

177

Conan the comedian. Conan the Barbarian!" I put
on my best Ah-nold Schwarzenegger voice. "'I am
Conan the Hurricane. I will huff and puff and blow
your tallest trees down.'"

The laughs grow bigger. A small crowd gathers
in a circle around me. There are some kids, so I pull
out a couple of corny one-liners I remember from
my floating joke books.

I turn to the man with the coffee cup. "What did one tornado say to the other?"

The man's smile widens. "Let's twist again like we did last summer."

More laughs. I pretend to be offended.

"Great. This is why I hate hurricanes. Everybody in the Red Cross shelter thinks they're a comedian."

"Yeah," says Mr. Coffee, "but ain't none of us ever been on TV with Ray What's-His-Name."

"Romano," I say. "Like the Italian cheese. I bet he's glad he isn't Ray Parmesan or Ray Mozzarella. Hey—anybody else hungry for pizza all of a sudden?"

You think I'm in bad shape? One time, back in the Old West, a three-legged dog walked into a saloon. He slid up to the bar and announced: "I'm looking for the man who shot my paw."

I do about thirty minutes of material.

Everybody is laughing and smiling, but eventually, I have to stop.

Kids need to go to sleep. The Red Cross needs to save gas in the generator and turn off the lights.

Soon it's very quiet again—except for the wind still whipping through the empty streets outside.

And some people sobbing.

People who've lost their homes, maybe worse.

I'm glad I was able to help them forget all that, if only for a few minutes.

Chapter 47

FUNNY MEETING YOU HERE

And then something funny happens.

Not *ha-ha* funny. More like *weird* funny.

The Gaynors and the Pierces arrive at the Red Cross shelter. Joey and his mom; Jimmy and his dad, mom, and little sister.

"I'm glad you're safe," says Pierce. "Hurricane Sam was a category four when it made landfall, the same as the great Galveston, Texas, hurricane disaster of September eighth to ninth, 1900."

"Awesome," says Gaynor.

Yep. My brainiac and headbanger buds are back, as if nothing ever happened—like, for instance, me turning into a jerk.

"You guys?" I say, mustering up the guts to apologize again.

"I already told them," says Gilda, coming over to complete our group hug.

So we hang out and shoot the bull like we used to, until, one by one, we all sort of drift off. Gaynor, Pierce, and Gilda go bunk down with their families. The Smileys curl up together and sleep. Yes, they frown when they dream, too.

I kind of conk out in my chair.

Until about three in the morning.

I feel a gentle nudge and creak open my eyes.

It's Uncle Frankie.

He's smiling at me.

The man who just lost his diner, his beloved boardwalk, his whole life, is smiling.

"Are you okay?" I ask.

"Yeah. How's by you, Jamie?"

"I'm good. I'm also sorry."

Uncle Frankie waves my apology away. "Fuhgeddaboudit. Water under the bridge. Water over the boardwalk, too. In fact, right now, there's so much water floating around town, I'm thinking about looking up SpongeBob. Maybe go live with him in that pineapple under the sea."

I can't believe it. Uncle Frankie is cracking jokes.

I guess comedy is always a good thing—even after a tragedy.

We find an empty cot.

"Good night, kiddo. Get some rest. Tomorrow will be better. Hey, it has to be."

PART TWO
Hooray for Hollywood?

Chapter 48

A VERY DARK MORNING

I roll out of the high school gym the next morning smiling because Uncle Frankie's words are still ringing in my ears: "Tomorrow will be better."

Or maybe not.

The town—no, make that my entire world—is a wreck.

The boardwalk is gone. Homes have been wiped out. Cars are buried up to their necks in sand. There are downed trees and dangling power lines everywhere. The National Guard is patrolling the streets to discourage looters.

Maybe this isn't the "tomorrow" Uncle Frankie was talking about. I have a feeling that one is more than a day away.

Chapter 49

LONG-DISTANCE DISTRESS

Long Beach Middle School is "closed until further notice."

So I spend my day hanging out at the shelter with Gilda, Gaynor, Pierce, and the Smileys. The Red Cross is amazing. We actually have Lucky Charms cereal for breakfast.

"We could've used these yesterday," I crack. "Because Hurricane Sam opened a box of Honey Bunches of Whoop-Butt."

I'm doing my best to cheer everybody up. That's, I guess, what comedians are supposed to do. We make people laugh so, for a couple of seconds, anyway, they can forget how miserable they really are.

If I'm really funny, maybe a few of my friends

and neighbors will forget that the hurricane turned their beachside bungalows into fast-sinking houseboats that floated away on the morning tide.

Pierce is able to rig up my laptop with Wi-Fi (don't ask me how), which is a good thing.

Until Judy Nazemetz hits me up with a Skype call. Then things get even worse.

"I may not go to the finals," she tells me.

"What? Why not?"

"My dad. He's very sick, Jamie. I have to fly out to see him in Oklahoma City."

"The one in Oklahoma?" I say because, basically, I don't know what else to say.

"Yeah," says Judy. "His doctors say he has, like, a week left to live. So the last thing I can do right now is think funny thoughts or work up new material."

I nod. I know the feeling. After Hurricane Sam, I really don't feel much like writing new jokes or prepping for the final round of the Planet's Funniest Kid Comic Contest, either.

"Maybe," I say, "because of the hurricane, they'll postpone the show. And if you tell them about your dad—"

On screen, I see Judy shake her head. "Joe Amodio, the executive producer, was on TV this morning. 'The show must go on,' he said. 'In times of tragedy, America needs comedy more than ever.' He says the whole country's counting on us to make them smile, if only for a couple of hours next week."

Yep. The finals are only, like, seven days away. Uncle Frankie and I are supposed to fly back to Hollywood the day after tomorrow.

"I guess, what with the hurricane wiping out Long Beach, you have to make the same kind of choice as me, huh, Jamie?" says Judy. "Fame or family. Which is more important?"

Technically, I don't have much family left. Just the Smileys. And Uncle Frankie. And my friends. So, yeah. I'm faced with the same horrible choice that Judy is.

"It's tough," I say.

"Maybe we should both sit this out."

I grin. "Well, I've got the chair for it."

She finally smiles. "You're a good guy, Jamie Grimm. Sweet, too."

"Thanks."

We end our call.

"Hey, Jamie," says Joey Gaynor, coming over with a lady in a Windbreaker who is being trailed by a guy in a poncho lugging a large video camera.

The lady is holding a microphone with some kind of local TV station logo slapped on its front—the same logo that's plastered all over her jacket.

"This is Buffy Barton. I told her you were here, dude. She's, like, a TV reporter."

"I *am* a TV reporter," says Ms. Barton. "Your friend Joey tells me you're one of the four funniest kids on the planet?"

I nod. Even though, after talking to Judy Nazemetz and hearing about her sick dad, the last thing I'm feeling is funny.

"Yes, ma'am. I'm Jamie Grimm."

The camera operator snaps on his blindingly bright halogen floodlight.

And, just like the big-time TV producer said, the show must go on.

Chapter 50

MAKE 'EM LAUGH

I'm here at a Long Beach hurricane shelter with Jamie Grimm," Buffy Barton tells the TV camera, "one of the four funny finalists in BNC's big million-dollar kid comedian contest. How are you holding up, Jamie?"

"We're going to be okay. My family is safe. My friends are all here. The Red Cross has been terrific."

"But you're the only celebrity bunking on the cots?"

"Actually, I heard a rumor that Ariel, the Little Mermaid, is here, too. She washed ashore in the storm surge. And Bruce, the shark from *Jaws*? He's in the kitchen helping them open chili cans with his teeth."

"See?" shouts Gaynor. "I told you. He funny."

The reporter nods. "We understand you have been performing for the hundreds of storm victims sheltered here in the high school gymnasium?"

"Yes, ma'am. And it's better than any nightclub in Las Vegas. None of those places have basketball hoops or roll-out bleachers."

And then, at the urging of my friends, I give Ms. Barton a few minutes of storm-related one-liners and other jokes.

That night, my little improv in the Long Beach hurricane shelter makes the local news in New York City.

And then, believe or not, the same piece is picked up by Aiden Buchholz for the BNC national news.

"In the aftermath of Hurricane Sam," Buchholz croons into the camera, "a plucky young kid comic is helping others make the best of an extremely bad situation."

By eight PM, I'm everywhere. Facebook. Blogs. I even have my very own hashtag on Twitter: #FUNNYHURRICANEKID.

This is a good thing, according to the Red Cross. Because of my little schtick in the storm shelter, charitable donations are through the roof. It's like my two-minute news clip was a mini-telethon, raising boatloads of money for the victims of Hurricane Sam.

I'm feeling great.

Until I receive another Skype call.

This one comes in around midnight. From Moose Lake, Minnesota.

Chapter 51

PUTTING THE "YIKES" INTO SKYPE

Yep. It's Chatty Patty Dombrowski.

"Judy Nazemetz gave me your Skype ID," she huffs into her webcam. She has one hand propped on her hip so she can lean into the screen and give me some major-league 'tude.

Okay. I guess I can forgive Judy for revealing my private Skype contact info. After all, Judy's grieving. Her father might be about to die.

"Seriously, Grimm," Patty sneers. "How many pity points are you trying to rack up, anyways?"

"Huh?"

"This publicity stunt with the hurricane."

"Stunt?"

"Cripes' sake, you're fame obsessed. You want to be famous and you're mad you're not."

"I'm sorry, Patty—"

"Real quick, Jamie—my name is Patricia. Especially when I'm upset."

"Well, what are you so upset about, Patricia?"

"*You!* Wasn't it enough for you to be the only crippled kid in the competition? Now you have to be some big, heroic hurricane survivor, too?"

"Oh, you mean that stuff on TV. That wasn't my idea. That was just—"

"Did you ever think about winning this contest just by being, oh, I don't know—FUNNY?"

"Honestly, Patricia—"

She puts on a pouty face and a crybaby voice and rubs both eyes with her balled-up fists. "Poor wittle Jamie Gwimm. He's in a wittle bitty wheelchair and all his friends got rained on real hard. Boo-hoo."

She's making me kind of mad now.

"Hey, guess what, Patricia? I may not even do the stupid show. Judy may drop out, too."

"Why?"

"Some things in life are more important than telling jokes."

"How would you know? You've never really told one, have you? You just roll out there and say, 'I'm sad and pathetic. Vote for me.'"

She hurls one insult after another at me.

"I'll never forget the first time we met, Jamie Grimm. But trust me, I'll keep trying."

I've had enough.

"Gee, Patricia. That joke's so old, the first time anybody said it the Dead Sea was still alive!"

"Um, was that supposed to be funny? Face it, if it wasn't for your wheelchair, you never would've made it all the way to the finals."

"Somebody could've carried me," I quip.

"Yeah. They could've flopped you up onstage like a wet walleye. Which is what you're gonna do anyways. Flop! So do us all a favor, why don'tcha? Quit whining about the gul-dern hurricane. You've already won the sympathy vote. Now try to earn a few laughs."

She clicks off.

I stare at the blank screen. And realize, once again, that Chatty Patty is correct.

I not funny.

I just handicapped.

And washed up.

MORE BAD NEWS
ON THE BOARDWALK

That night, Uncle Frankie cooks everybody free burgers on a barbecue grill the National Guard sets up in the high school parking lot.

"Had to clean out the refrigerator, kiddo," he tells me. "Without electricity, all my meat will go bad fast. All the ice cream in the freezer has already turned into soup."

"Really?" I say, hoping I can make him smile. "Forget cream of broccoli. Cream of ice cream has always been my favorite soup."

Uncle Frankie flips a burger and cracks a small smile.

I notice he's not spinning his yo-yo tonight.

"Is the diner going to be okay?" I ask.

All he can do is shrug. "We'll see, Jamie. Need to talk to the insurance people. And the folks from FEMA, the Federal Emergency Management Agency. I need to check in with a couple of people from the Governor's Hurricane Task Force, too. See if I can work out some kind of quick loan to get back on my feet. Then I'll go look for my jukebox. I think *all* the records in it right now are 'Under the Boardwalk.'"

My turn to smile. Uncle Frankie is making a joke because he has nothing in his jukebox but 1950s and '60s doo-wop music, including the classic hit "Under the Boardwalk" by a group called the Drifters.

"We'll get through this thing, Uncle Frankie."

"Sure we will, kiddo. We always do, am I right?"

"Yeah."

Now I'm thinking I *have* to do the show in Hollywood.

And, more importantly, I have to win.

Don't forget—the winner takes home one million dollars. That's enough money to help Uncle Frankie rebuild his diner *and* his doo-wop collection.

BACK TO SCHOOL...
AND SUDDENLY COOL

Good news—sort of.

School is open again. After three days of cot city, there's no place like homeroom.

We're back in school, but school isn't really back in, if you catch my drift. Most of the teachers live on Long Island, so they're dealing with their own Sam-related realities. Everybody's kind of shell-shocked—maybe from all the seashells the storm left behind.

So, basically, the educational content of our first day back is zip. Zero. *Nada.* (That was Spanish class.)

But after school, I am presented with a very interesting educational opportunity.

"Hey, Jamie." It's Matthew-Lucas Morrissey, one of the coolest kids in the school, probably because he has two first names. That's *super*cool. We're in the hall after the final bell rings.

"Uh, hi, Matthew-Lucas. Am I blocking your way?"

"Nope. We were wondering…"

Suddenly, half a dozen, maybe more, of the extremely coolest kids in all of Long Beach Middle School, maybe all of Long Island, have me surrounded.

"We want you to come to our party!" blurts Bianca-Whitney Matthews. Yeah. A lot of the extremely popular kids in Long Beach have more than one name.

"It's going to be superhot," says Gena Zagoren. She's a cheerleader. And, get this, she's talking to *me*.

"It's going to be a real posthurricane blowout," says Matthew-Lucas.

"Because the winds, like, 'blew out' people's windows and junk," says cheerleader Gena.

Matthew-Lucas and Bianca-Whitney are both nodding like crazy.

"My mom bought all sorts of soda and chips and cake and junk someplace where the grocery stores still have food," says Matthew-Lucas. "Even ice cream that isn't melted. This party is going to be awesome, Jamie. Totally off the hook."

Wow. I've never been invited to a cool kids' party before. I don't know how to react.

"And, uh, you guys want *me* to come to this party?"

"Wouldja?" squeals Bianca-Whitney. She's hopping up and down and clapping her fingertips together real fast. "That would be amazing."

"Yeah," says Matthew-Lucas. "You're a total TV star."

"You're my hero," says Gena, kicking her heel all the way up to her butt—the way cheerleaders do at the end of every routine.

I can feel my head slowly inflating like it's a beach ball.

Then I remember that I'm supposed to meet up with Gilda, Pierce, and Gaynor after school. Gaynor's mom, who's recovering from cancer, needs some prescriptions filled, and we planned to trek over to the pharmacy in the next town. But they'd understand. A once-in-a-lifetime opportunity to party with double-named cool kids only comes along, uh, once in a lifetime.

"Sure," I say. "Sounds like fun. I'm sure the food will be better than what the Red Cross has on the menu tonight: freeze-dried crud on a cracker."

All the cool kids crack up like that's the funniest thing they've ever heard.

"Come on, Jamie," says Bianca-Whitney. "My mom's outside with her SUV. I'll push you to the parking lot."

"Okay, but just don't talk about me behind my back."

Everybody busts a gut laughing at my recycled joke.

"You're funny!" squeals Gena.

Yes. Yes, I am.

HAULING MY BIG HEAD HOME

Around nine o'clock, Bianca-Whitney Matthews's mom drops me off back at the shelter.

I'm stuffed. The party was amazing. They had sheet cake and Moose Tracks ice cream and those Cool Ranch Doritos Locos Tacos from Taco Bell. I think I guzzled two liters of Mountain Dew. Every time I burp, I smell like a bowl of chili.

"Thanks for the ride, Mrs. Matthews," I say when I'm back in my wheelchair outside the high school gym.

"You're welcome, Jamie!" She does the giddy fingertip clap from behind the steering wheel. Guess that's where her daughter learned it.

"Come on, Jamie," pleads Bianca-Whitney. "One more joke. You're flying off to Hollywood tomorrow and you need to make me laugh one more time before I let you go!"

My smile's getting queasier and queasier, but I power forward.

"Okay. Um, a couple of months ago, I went to the Handicapped Olympics. Now, I don't want to point any fingers and call somebody a cheat, but come on—nobody should be slam-dunking in wheelchair basketball."

Bianca-Whitney and her mom yuk it up something fierce. But—and I'm being honest here—neither one laughs half as good as Gilda Gold.

But I have a funny feeling Gilda isn't talking to me again.

Gaynor and Pierce, either.

Guess it was pretty jerkish of me to ditch them and head off to a supercool party where all anybody wanted to hear were wheelchair jokes and how many celebrities I met while I was in LA. I think I told that same slam-dunking joke about six different times and promised to get Ray Romano's autograph for everybody. Guess Ray Romano's gonna hate me, too.

I roll into the Red Cross shelter.

"You're late," says Mrs. Smiley.

I play dumb. "Really? What time is it?"

"Nine-fifteen," says Mr. Smiley.

"You were supposed to be here by seven," adds Mrs. Smiley. "Everybody was, Jamie."

"I guess I lost track of the time."

I spent five minutes fixing my broken watch. At least I think it was five minutes.

"Where were you? You told everyone you'd do another show tonight. For the kids."

I try to shrug that off as if it's no big deal. "Hey, I was at a party."

Mrs. Smiley looks puzzled. "A party? Who in Long Beach has anything to celebrate?"

"Me," I say. "And all the cool kids at school. It was my big send-off for Hollywood. It's not every day that somebody from Long Beach Middle School makes it all the way to the Final Four."

Mr. Smiley looks confused. "You're playing basketball?"

Mrs. Smiley helps him out. "The comedy contest, dear. Jamie and Frankie are supposed to fly out to Los Angeles again, first thing tomorrow morning."

"Yeah. I'm sad to go." I open my arms to take in all the people camping out on cots. "I'm gonna miss all this."

Yes, I'm being sarcastic.

And a little mean-spirited.

That's the dark side of comedy. When you use it as a weapon to defend yourself, you can also injure innocent bystanders.

In fact, once, not too long ago, I made a vow that I would never, ever tell a joke if it hurt somebody other than me.

But that was before I made it to the Final Four.

And all the coolest kids at school wanted me to make them laugh.

And Chatty Patty reminded me how not funny I am.

And Uncle Frankie needed a million bucks to reopen his diner and buy a new jukebox.

Mrs. Smiley sighs and looks sadder than I've ever seen a Smiley, which is saying something.

"We're very disappointed in you, Jamie," she says.

"I know. Excuse me."

I roll off to the restrooms to be by myself and stare at someone else who's seriously disappointed in my behavior today.

Me.

Chapter 55

STINKING UP THE BATHROOM

My smartphone has a flashlight app.

So I flick it on and pretend I'm out in Hollywood, basking in the spotlight, even though I'm in the high school locker room, gacking in the stench of a thousand soggy sweat socks.

Before I fly off to Hollywood for the finals, I have to make sure I'm ready to rock.

I need my best material. Nothing but my A-game.

No more lame wheelchair jokes. To win this thing, I need primo Jamie Grimm-o.

Too bad I've got absolutely nothing. It's zip, zero, *nada* time again.

I turn away from the mirrors and stare at all the doors to the toilet stalls. I can't even come up with a single decent knock-knock joke.

Nothing's working. Nothing's funny.

Except the idea that I ever thought I could be a big-time comedian. *That's* hilarious. Which reminds me of the only joke I can remember right now: "People laughed at me when I told them I was going to be a comedian. Well, they're not laughing now."

Totally dejected, I roll out of the locker room and head for my cot.

As I drift off to sleep, I squeeze my eyes tight

and say a silent prayer: "Um, God, it's me again. Jamie Grimm. Uh, sir, if you haven't given up on me already—and to tell the truth, I wouldn't blame you if you had—can you throw me a bone, here? A funny bone? Just one joke? Maybe something about you and Moses golfing up in heaven with your son? Or how about something zany at the Pearly Gates with Saint Peter?"

I wait.

All I hear are snores and creaking cots.

Seems God is all out of fresh material for me, too.

So I ask Him for one last favor.

"Please tell Mom and Dad and little Jenny that I'm sorry for turning into an egomaniacal bonehead. I think I need to apologize to you, too, sir. I'm sorry I took this gift you gave me and blew it. I really, truly am. And if you ever give me another gift, I promise—I'll take better care of it. Thank you, sir."

Chapter 56

WAKE-UP CALL

The next morning, I wake up to somebody screaming my name.

"Jamie Grimm? Mr. Jamie Grimm!"

To stop him from shouting (and rhyming), I wave at him.

"Wow!" he hollers. "You're *that* Jamie Grimm!"

Now everybody in the whole shelter is awake.

I figure they hate me for ruining their sleep (and for being the kind of nitwit twit who goes to an ice-cream-and-cake party when they're all eating government-surplus cheese and baked beans out of tin cans).

But, surprise—these people *don't* hate me. They see the limo driver and figure out what's going on.

"Go get 'em, Jamie!" somebody shouts.

"Make 'em laugh, Jamie!" hollers somebody else. "Tell 'em that joke you told us the other night!"

"You funny!"

Now applause starts up. A smattering of claps at first, but it builds into a thunderous ovation. People are on their feet. Kids are banging empty bean cans against the metal frames of their beds.

The cheering and chanting builds.

"I won't let you guys down!" I promise.

And this time I mean it.

I transfer myself into the limo and we head off for Uncle Frankie's diner. He's been sleeping at his restaurant ever since the storm. "Just so I can keep my eye on things," he says. "Not that there are too many things left for me to keep an eye on anymore."

The diner looks so sad. And it used to rival Disney World as the happiest place on earth.

But Uncle Frankie soldiers on.

"Tomorrow's a bright new day, kiddo. Just like it always is."

Chapter 57

SWIMMING WITH THE HOLLYWOOD SHARKS

There's an even bigger limousine waiting for us when we reach LAX, which is what they call the airport out in Los Angeles.

"Courtesy of Mr. Max Weasley and all the talent agents at WWW eager to work with you, Mr. Grimm," says the limo driver. He even clicks his heels for extra emphasis.

"Who's this Weasley character?" Uncle Frankie asks while the driver hauls our luggage to the trunk.

"A big-shot Hollywood talent agent," I tell him. "We met when I did *The Tonight Show* with Jimmy Fallon."

"He a good guy?"

"Hard to say."

"He sent you a limo, didn't he?" says the driver, who's finished loading our bags. "I'd say that makes him a swell guy, wouldn't you?"

Uncle Frankie peers at the driver. "I guess we can go hear him out. No harm in that."

"I'm told there will be a tray of baked goods awaiting your arrival," says the driver. "Including those brownies that taste like chocolate chip cookies."

"They call those blondies," I say.

"Oooh," says Uncle Frankie. "I like blondes. Let's roll."

We head for the West Star Building, home to the WWW (Weasley, Weeble & Weezer) Talent Agency.

"Grimm baby! How are you, *bubelah*?"

Max Weasley greets us in a conference room filled with high-powered agents, all of them wearing sleek suits and hip, chunky glasses. There are trays of pastries on the table. Uncle Frankie grabs a blondie.

"Flight okay, Jamie baby?"

"Yes, sir," I say.

"Just a little jet-lagged," adds Uncle Frankie.

Max Weasley pushes a button on an intercom box. "Helga? Send in a cappuccino, a double espresso, and a toffee nut, vanilla soy, no whip, extra foam, two-pump mocha for me."

"You want a soda, Jamie?" says one of the other agents. "We could get you a soda. We could get you a whole soda machine." He pushes the intercom button. "Mary? Have Fred down in maintenance grab a hand truck and roll the Coke machine into conference room C. Unless you prefer Pepsi, Jamie?"

"Er, that's okay," I say, wondering why everyone in LA is so weird. "I'm not all that thirsty."

"But are you hungry?" says Weasley, shooting me a wink.

"Grab a blondie," suggests Uncle Frankie. "They're good. Very chewy."

"I'm talking about the real hunger," says Max Weasley, slapping his stomach. "The fire in your belly. The hunger for fame and fortune! Gang? Show this wonderful wunderkind what we've already got lined up for him the second he signs on the dotted line." He snaps his fingers. One by one, the junior agents flip up presentations mounted on foam board.

They bombard us with one unbelievably amazing promise after another.

It gets me thinking. What would I do or want if it were up to me? What would I promise myself?

"So, Jamie baby?" Max Weasley's gruff voice snaps me out of my daydream. "You ready to sign up with WWW?"

I'm about to shout YES when Uncle Frankie holds up his hand.

"I'm Jamie's legal guardian while he's out here. He needs to sleep on it."

"You're his uncle Frankie, am I right?" says Max Weasley.

"That's right."

"Former yo-yo champion of Brooklyn?"

"The same."

"Guys?" Max Weasley snaps his fingers again.

Now all the agents hold up posters detailing their plans for Uncle Frankie. His own yo-yo show on the Home Hobby Network. A fast-food chain called Yo-Yo's where all the food is round and comes with a string so you never lose it. Yo-Yo's string cheese. Yo-Yo's yogurt.

Uncle Frankie smiles. "Nice try, guys. But, like I said, Jamie needs to sleep on it."

Chapter 58

SLEEPING LIKE A BABY: CRYING AND SCREAMING ALL NIGHT

That night I actually do sleep.

And since we're in Hollywood, my dream features a movie. It's running backward and it's all about me.

Me eating cake and ice cream with the supercool kids back in Long Beach.

Me ignoring Gaynor and Pierce in the cafeteria. And in the library. And on the way home.

Me kissing Judy Nazemetz on national TV even though I know Gilda Gold is watching.

Me with such a big head, Goodyear hires me to fly over football games.

Me telling nothing but wheelchair jokes so everybody will feel sorry for me.

And then, since this is a dream and the movie is running in reverse, I finally see its title.

There's no one else in the movie theater. Just me.

I can't blame everybody for walking out on my life story. I just wish I could join them.

Early the next morning, there's a knock on my hotel room door.

More like a banging. Somebody with a sledgehammer fist is pounding on it hard. It definitely wakes me up.

"Yes?" I mumble groggily as I pull myself across the bed toward my wheelchair.

"It's your bodyguard, Crip. Let me in. Or else!"

Chapter 59

A LITTLE NY IN LA

The TV people wanted us to be in the studio audience cheering for you," says Stevie as he swaggers into my room. "So they flew us out, first class. But I am not, repeat, NOT, holding up some kind of dorky sign like those families you always see in the crowd on *American Idol*."

"I brought you some fresh, homemade oat gruel," says Mrs. Smiley, handing me a Tupperware bowl. "You'll need a good breakfast tomorrow to be good and funny for the show."

"Had a heck of a time getting the oat gruel past security," adds Mr. Smiley. I nod. I've had Mrs. Smiley's oat glop every morning for many a month. It is a potentially lethal weapon.

"We brought a security dog, too," says Stevie,

my bodyguard. "In case I need backup."

Ol' Smiler comes plodding into the room. He sniffs the closet and drags out the fancy hotel bathrobe. After nosing it around in circles on the floor to make a comfy dog bed, he flops down to take a nap. Guess the six-hour flight in a doggy crate wore him out.

Stevie's little brother and sister made the trip, too.

Wow. Since Uncle Frankie flew out to Los Angeles with me and the Smileys are here now, my whole family (except for second cousins once removed, whatever those are) will be in the audience for the finals.

I'm not in this thing alone. I guess I never really have been, have I?

For the first time since forever, I feel great. I'm a new man! Just like Ebenezer Scrooge waking up on Christmas morning. I know my life doesn't have to end up miserably. How it turns out is up to me. I can be a changed man if I just, you know, make a few changes.

Like not acting like a jerk, for starters.

Around ten AM Hollywood time, I prop open my laptop, hook up with the hotel's Wi-Fi network, and make a quick Skype call to my friends back at Long Beach Middle School. It's three hours later in New York, so I know they'll be in the library.

Pierce always has his smartphone up and running (in stealthy silent mode, of course), so I Skype with him and Gaynor. I want to tell them both how sorry I am for continuing to act like an idiot even after I promised I would quit acting idiotical.

When we're all cool again, Gaynor and Pierce run down the hall to find Gilda so she and I can have a little face time, too.

"I'm sorry" are the first words out of my mouth.

"What?" says Gilda. "You don't say hello anymore?"

And, since Gilda and I first bonded over old Marx Brothers movies, I answer her question by singing a quick verse of Groucho Marx's classic "Hooray for Captain Spaulding" song from the 1930 movie *Animal Crackers*.

"*Hello, I must be going. I cannot stay, I came to say, I must be going.*

I'm glad I came, but just the same, I must be going. La la."

And then I wiggle my eyebrows, Groucho-style. Gilda is grinning.

"I'm sorry," I tell Gilda. I take a deep breath before I say what I need to say. I know I'm going to sound stupid, but real friends don't hold that against you. "It's no excuse, but, well, I think I'm afraid."

"Of what?"

"Oh, let's see. Failing on the biggest stage in the universe. Losing the Super Bowl of kid comedians. Whiffing in the World Series of yuks. What if I'm not funny? What if I really am just a big jerk on wheels?"

"So write your act around that. How a nice kid became a cocky, totally obnoxious, fame-crazy comic."

I nod. And think. And nod some more.

"Gee. I kinda love that idea."

"I know," says Gilda. "I'm a genius."

"You're not getting cocky, are you?"

"No, Jamie. That's your department."

"Correction," I say. "That *was* my department."

Now we both laugh.

You know what? Laughing at myself feels good. Really, really good.

Chapter 60

STRESS REHEARSAL

Fired up, I head off to the Nokia Theatre with Uncle Frankie.

That's right. The final round of the Planet's Funniest Kid Comic Contest will take place in the same ginormous, seven-thousand-seat auditorium where they hold the *American Idol* finals and the American Music Awards.

Chatty Patty Dombrowski and Antony Guerrero are there with their adult chaperones. One looks like Patty's mom, the other like Antony's dad.

Patty also has what they call an entourage. She's like a princess being followed around by fawning, flattering attendants. If this were a fairy tale, they'd all be wearing those pointy hats with silk scarves stuck on the tips. I think she brought

her agent and her manager, not to mention her wardrobe, hair, and makeup people, too.

I don't see Judy Nazemetz. She hasn't been on Skype lately, so I don't know if she'll be here. I hope she's just running late.

"The show's going out live tomorrow night, kids," says our director, a goateed guy named Mr. Russell. "We need to block out the camera moves and show you kids how to hit your marks. We also need to pull numbers to determine the order you'll be going on in."

Ray Romano and the celebrity judges aren't at the rehearsal. Their stand-ins or stunt doubles or whatever they're called take their places.

"Where's my Judy Nazemetz?" the director barks.

"Send Ms. Nazemetz's double to the set," his assistant barks to his walkie-talkie.

"Sending her in," the walkie-talkie barks back with a burst of static.

"We'll rehearse the show as if Judy's in it, but we have to be prepared for her to drop out at the last minute," explains the director. "She may not be here tomorrow night. She's dealing with a major family emergency."

Her father, I think. I'm guessing Judy is still in Oklahoma City.

Chatty Patty raises her hand. "Golly, if Judy isn't here tomorrow, does that mean there will only be three of us in the Final Four?"

"That's right. The math's a little screwy, but, hey—we gotta work with what we got, am I right?" The director's assistant hands him a three-ring binder. Mr. Russell flips forward a few pages. "Okay. It's a two-hour show. You're each scheduled to do a fifteen-minute routine. However, if Ms. Nazemetz is a no-show, you need to stretch your fifteen to twenty minutes and give me a big laugh line at the fifteen-minute mark so we can cut to a commercial."

"No problem," mumbles Antony Guerrero, who, even though he is loud and brash onstage, is one of the shiest, quietest kids I've ever met. "Sorry about your friend Judy," he says to me.

"Yeah. Me too. Thanks."

"Golly," gushes Patty, batting her big-as-cue-balls eyes at the director. "I could do more jokes if you need them. Why, I could do a whole half hour."

"Thanks, kid. You're sweet. But if we need even more filler, we'll handle it with Ray and the judges. Okay, you three need to draw numbers out of a hat." He turns to his assistant again. "Where's my hat?"

"On your head, sir."

"What's it doing there? We need to be drawing numbers!"

"Yes, sir. Right away, sir."

The assistant plucks the baseball cap off Mr. Russell's head.

The assistant's assistant scribbles numbers on four slips of paper. The assistant's assistant's assistant takes the numbers and jumbles them up inside the hat.

Then the assistants hand the hat back to each other until the first assistant hands it back to the director.

"Okay, kids. Pick a number."

Antony reaches in and pulls out number two.

Chatty Patty yanks out number one and does an arm pump. "Yes!" she exclaims. "Lucky number one. Again!"

I reach in and pull out my folded slip of paper.

Number four.

Once again, I'm going on last.

Which means, if she makes it back to Hollywood in time, I'll be going onstage right after Judy Nazemetz.

Chapter 61

CHANGING MY ACT
IN MIDSTREAM

Okay," says the director, "I need you each to give me two or three minutes of material so we can set sound and light levels."

We rehearse in the order we'll perform in the show.

Chatty Patty races to center stage, grabs the microphone, and starts cracking up everybody on the crew with her "dumb" act. She's really good. She could definitely win.

"Thanks, Ms. Dombrowski," booms the director's voice from out in the darkened auditorium. "That's all we need for now. Antony? You're up next."

The other day, my teacher asked us, "What's brown and sticky?" I said, "A stick."

Patty hurries offstage and finds a seat in the auditorium. She pulls out a pen and paper.

Is she going to write down all Antony Guerrero's jokes and try to steal them?

She'll be the first one onstage, so if she does one of Antony's one-liners, he'll have to change his act on the fly or everybody will think he stole his jokes from Patty. The same will be true for me.

Antony sees Patty and her notepad out in the auditorium, too.

"Don't give her your A material," he whispers to me. "Save it for tomorrow."

He heads to center stage and does a very funny riff on why Mexican-Americans get so confused at Taco Bell.

"Wow, a taco shell that tastes like Cool Ranch Doritos. It's just like Mamá used to make. Of course, my mother has a PhD in chemical engineering. Nachos Bell Grande? Very interesting meal. You get to eat the bowl because it's a big scooped-out tortilla chip. We used to do this at my grandfather's house. All his bowls were edible. His cups, too. In fact, everything in his whole house was made out of tortilla chips—just like that old fairy tale about the lady who lived in the gingerbread house, only spicier. We used to go over there and nibble on the furniture. 'Antony, are you *loco*?' Grandpa used to yell at me. 'How we gonna watch football? You ate the TV!'"

Wow. If that's not his A material, I'm in big trouble. The guy is hysterical.

"Jamie Grimm?" calls the director. "Do you need help getting onstage?"

"No, sir," I say, and roll my way out into the spotlight.

I start out sort of slow because I'm kind of

rewriting my act as I go, trying to do like Gilda suggested. Just tell my story. Just be me.

Hi, I'm Jamie Grimm. And you're probably wondering how I ended up on this stage. I mean, not many professional ballet dancers do stand-up comedy, too. So, yeah, I was in a car accident. Can't use my legs. Except, you know, to wear my pants. Needed someplace to keep my shoes, too.

The director cuts me off after a couple of minutes.

I push my chair offstage.

Antony Guerrero gives me a "nice" nod. "I like where you're going. Keep it up, man."

"That was good, Jamie," says Uncle Frankie, who's waiting for me in the wings. "A good start. I definitely think you're heading in the right direction."

"Too bad the big show's tomorrow night. This probably isn't the best time to be finally finding my new direction. It might be too little, too late."

Uncle Frankie doesn't argue with me.

"It's okay," I say. "I get it. I did this to myself."

Chapter 62

EVEN MORE HOTEL GUESTS

When Uncle Frankie and I get back to the hotel, the Smileys aren't the only ones hanging out in my room.

Max Weasley and all those talent agents from WWW have joined them.

"So, Jamie baby," says the super-agent, "are you ready to sign our little agreement?"

"Well, uh…"

"We're still thinking about your offer, Mr. Weasley," says Uncle Frankie.

"Sure. But while you're thinking about it, think about this: You sign with us, we'll buy you a new house. A mansion. In Beverly Hills. I'm talking 90210!"

While the agents are making their pitch, the Smileys are staring at them silently.

They're in full-on frown mode.

And it's kind of freaking out all the Hollywood people.

Chapter 63

PARTY? ON A SCHOOL NIGHT?

Soooo," says Max, bringing his hand to the side of his mouth. "Who are these sourpusses?"

"Oh, I'm sorry. I should've introduced you. That's my aunt, my other uncle, my three cousins—"

"I'm also his bodyguard," growls Stevie.

"Beautiful," says Mr. Weasley. "So, you folks must be superproud of Jamie, am I right?"

The Smileys (except Stevie, of course) nod a bit.

"How'd you like to have your own mansion next door to Jamie's mansion?"

Now they sort of shrug.

"We'll give you all cars, too. Even the kids. Them, we'll give go-carts. Or Hot Wheels. Do kids still like Hot Wheels? How about that iPad car racing game? We'll give you iPads, too."

No reaction. Nothing.

"Just smile. Or scream."

Max Weasley is practically begging.

"Do something. Anything. Please. I'm in showbiz. I need constant feedback from people I don't really know. I also need huge fees, like twenty-five percent of everything Jamie ever makes. Actually, you can reverse that order. I need the fees first."

Still nothing.

No reaction from the Smileys.

And no signed contract from me.

"Hey," says Max Weasley, totally flustered, "how would you folks like to come to a little party at my place tonight?"

"Little?" scoffs one of the other agents. "It'll be the biggest, most spectacular Hollywood party *ever*."

"Jamie can sign the contract at the party," says Max Weasley. "It'll be a celebration. All about you, Jamie baby, and your big, bright, boffo future."

"But," I say, "the finals are tomorrow. I really shouldn't go to a party. I need to get to bed early. I can't—"

Stevie Kosgrov shows me the palm of his hand.

"We'll be there, Max baby," he says. "And don't worry, dead or alive, Jamie's coming, too!"

HEARD ANY JUICY HOLLYWOOD GOSSIP LATELY?

I really don't want to go to the Hollywood party, but Uncle Frankie thinks it might be a good idea.

"You need to relax, kiddo. I learned this back when I was on the yo-yo tourney circuit. It's always good to unwind a little before you have to wind your string up tight for the big show."

Then I make a major mistake.

After I dress for the party, I Google myself to find out how America thinks I'll fare in the final round of the competition. One click and I'm bombarded with 2,362,014 results in 0.37 seconds.

Every one of those results is a juicy rumor that, apparently, is swarming all over cyberspace as it zips across Twitter, Facebook, Instagram, Tumblr, Pinterest, and even Google+.

The rumor with more juice than Jamba?

That I can walk.

That my legs aren't really paralyzed.

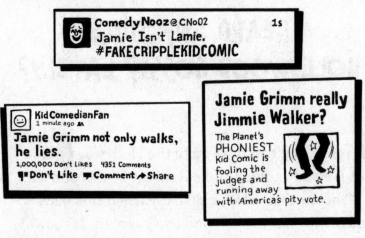

To make matters worse, they have proof. Photographs of me walking, running, swimming, and, yes, dancing.

The blogs are unbelievably nasty.

Most suggest I should drop out of the competition before the final round. "Jamie Grimm should walk away from the spotlight now. Literally. He should get up out of that chair and just walk off the stage and back to Nobodyville where he belongs!"

There's only one problem with this juicy rumor.

Well, two.

First, it's not true. This is why I am currently lying on the floor like a resident of a roach motel. I thought I'd see if maybe I *could* walk and just forgot.

I can't.

Second, all those pictures? Not a single one of them was taken *after* the car wreck.

The accident that put me in my chair.

Chapter 65

A MOB OF REPORTERS

Now we're kind of trapped inside the hotel.

The media, chasing the news about my phony handicap, have arrived and set up camp downstairs in the lobby and outside in the parking lot.

From my window, I can see satellite dishes on top of TV trucks and an angry mob of reporters shouting at the building. They remind me of the mob in my favorite Mel Brooks movie, *Young Frankenstein*. Only, they're jabbing the air with microphones instead of pitchforks.

"Um, you guys?" I say to the Smileys and Uncle Frankie. "Maybe you should go to Mr. Weasley's party without me. A mob can be an ugly thing."

"That crowd down there isn't ugly," says Stevie. "They're all TV reporters."

"With very nice hair," adds Mrs. Smiley. "And excellent teeth. I'm sure their dentists are proud."

"Still," I say, "no way am I rolling through that pack of wolves."

"You won't have to," says Uncle Frankie with a sly grin. "We'll do the rolling for you!"

Chapter 66

MY NEW WHEELCHAIR

So Uncle Frankie, Mr. Smiley, and Stevie stuff me inside a rolling suitcase.

"Use your arms to tuck your knees up to your chin and try not to breathe too much," suggests Uncle Frankie as he zips up the bag.

Fortunately for me, it's a jumbo-sized piece of luggage. (I think it's the one Stevie used to pack all his torture equipment for the trip out west.)

So this is what it feels like to be a pretzel.

Mrs. Smiley takes my wheelchair. She pretends she sprained her ankle and can't walk on it. Since all the reporters are looking for me, not the Smileys or Uncle Frankie, we're able to sneak down to the lobby and out to where another stretch limousine is waiting for us. Yes, I'll have to ride in the trunk. But only for a block or two. When we're safely away from the hotel mob, Uncle Frankie promises we'll pull over and make another switcheroo.

"Unless we forget," says Stevie, who I think is going to add the Suitcase Sauna Squeeze to his list of all-pro bullying techniques.

Anyway, the luggage-cram scam works. We waltz right past the press and the paparazzi.

Chapter 67

PIN THE TAIL
ON THE MOVIE STAR

Max was right. The big Hollywood party is absolutely amazing.

Everybody who is anybody is there, including people who used to be nobodies—like me.

I'm gawking at the celebrities and collecting all sorts of autographs.

Meanwhile, the Smileys couldn't care less. They're spending all their time staring at the fancy food.

"Who wants vegan pizza with pesto grilled vegetables?" grumbles Stevie. "I want an In-N-Out burger. I hear they're the best in LA."

Max Weasley comes up to me.

He's shaking his head and reading something on his smartphone.

"You can walk?"

"No, sir. That's just—"

"Jamie baby. *Bubelah*. Sweetheart. You lied to me? You lied to Max Weasley?"

"No, sir. I—"

"I'm withdrawing my offer to represent you."

"B-b-but—"

He holds up his hand. "Please, Jamie. No butt jokes. They're so last week. Excuse me. I have to go sign up some major new talent: the Smileys! Those people are amazing. No one in Hollywood has ever seen anything like 'em!"

He hustles over to where one of the Kardashian sisters is trying to get Mr. Smiley's attention.

It's no use.

He's busy peeling vegetables off the top of a mini-pizza. "Where's the pepperoni, sausage, and bacon?"

"It's vegan," explains Mrs. Smiley. "It's all vegetables."

"Even the cheese?" complains Mr. Smiley. "That's weird."

None of the Smileys are paying any attention to the high-wattage megastars surrounding them. They're focused on the food. And the ice sculptures.

"That statue might melt," says Mrs. Smiley. "His nose is already dripping."

They are more interested in frozen hunks of water than all the celebs.

And the movie stars love it.

Yes, suddenly, the Smileys are hot.

Max Weasley offers the Smileys their own TV show. Their own movie. A record deal. Commercial endorsements.

All the stuff that, twenty-four hours ago, he offered me.

Chapter 68

RAFE TO THE RESCUE

Hold on. Wait a second. Attitude adjustment time.

I see one of my all-time favorite stars on the other side of the swimming pool.

Rafe Khatchadorian! The middle school maniac!

"What are you doing in Hollywood?" I ask Rafe.

I love this angle! I'm a genius! Hey, kid in the wheelchair? Don't fall into the swimming pool! Not until I shout "Action!"

"I had an idea for that sign up in the hills. We could rearrange the letters, make it spell *Doh Woolly*. Everybody will think Homer Simpson did it. D'oh!"

"I think he's here at the party."

"Cool," says Rafe. "Love to meet Homer."

I nod. "Me too. Because right now, I agree with what he told Bart: 'Trying is the first step toward failure.' My act is a mess. I need to rewrite the whole thing. By tomorrow."

"Hey," says Rafe, "for what it's worth, I still believe in you, Jamie."

"You do?"

"Definitely."

"But why?"

"Because, uh, you know—I, being me, still believe in you, being you. See, I believed in you before and now, uh, I still do."

"Seriously? That's your reason?"

Rafe shrugs. "Sorry, Jamie. This is Hollywood. I'm an actor. The writers give me lines, I say them. By the way, I love Gilda's idea for your act. Riffing on how you sort of turned into a jerk."

"Is this another line your writers wrote for you?"

"No. That one was from the heart. Listen to Gilda, Jamie. She hasn't steered you wrong yet."

Chapter 69

HEY, IT'S HOLLYWOOD. EVERYBODY'S A PHONY!

The next morning, my day starts with another buzzkill news blast.

But this one isn't about me.

My "friend"—the one I've been feeling sorry for, Judy Nazemetz—is on the BNC *Morning Show*. With her manager.

Who, by the way, also just happens to be her father.

That's right.

The same father who, she told me, was seriously sick somewhere in Oklahoma.

For the record, Mr. Nazemetz looks extremely healthy. Judy? She looks extremely crafty and cunning.

"I think my little girl has a good shot at winning the contest and taking home that one-million-dollar prize and another sitcom," says Mr. Nazemetz, reminding everybody what's at stake in the finals. "We've been at a secret, secluded location, rehearsing with her comedy coach. America is going to laugh its head off when it hears Judy's new material."

I think about that for a second.

Does America even have a head that it can laugh off? Would that be Maine?

"Give 'em a free sample, honey," says Mr. Nazemetz.

"Oh, that'd be terrific," says Pam Johnston, one of the *Morning Show* anchors.

"You want free?" says Judy. "Well, this prisoner, who's been locked up for years and years, is finally released. He runs around yelling, 'I'm free! I'm free!'

"A little kid walks up to him and says, 'So what? I'm four.'"

Anchorwoman Pam Johnston is cracking up. "Judy Nazemetz, you are one funny young woman!"

She's also one *sneaky* young woman.

The BNC *Morning Show* says good-bye to Judy and her dad. I flip open my laptop, do a quick self-Google, and guess what?

There are absolutely no new or snarky stories about me "walking." No new photos documenting my fraud.

I wheel over to look out the window.

Yep. The mob of reporters has gone home. I am definitely yesterday's news. Nobody even cares.

I type in Judy's Skype address. She actually answers.

"Hi!" she says. "Guess where I am?"

"Um, backstage at the BNC *Morning Show* studios?"

"Oh, you saw me?"

"Uh, yeah. And your father."

"He's my manager."

"I know. I heard. I thought he was busy in Oklahoma being sick."

I just roll my eyes. "Judy, why did you lie to me like that?"

"Because I lied to everybody else and didn't want to leave you out. We're friends."

"What?"

"I told Chatty Patty and Antony Guerrero the same fib about my dad. It was no biggie. I was just looking for a little edge in the competition."

"You wanted the three of us to waste our time working up a bunch of new material to fill in for you instead of concentrating on tightening our solid fifteen-minute routines?"

"Psych! Gotcha."

"That's horrible, Judy."

"No, Jamie. It's Hollywood. That's just the way the game is played. Nothing personal."

"But you already have your own TV show."

"So? If I win the competition, I'll get another one. Two is better than one, Jamie. Always."

"Did you spread that fake rumor, too?" I ask. "About me being able to walk?"

"Of course not." She waits a beat. "That was Chatty Patty's idea. We still friends?"

She smiles.

"I guess. I dunno. Sure."

Yeah. It's my turn to lie.

Told you so. By the way, I'm not gloating. Okay. I am gloating. A little.

275

Chapter 70

READY OR NOT, HERE I GO!

And so the big night finally arrives.

The Nokia Theatre is packed. Uncle Frankie and the Smileys are out in the audience, holding up signs and cheering me on.

Ray Romano does a quick monologue and introduces our celebrity judges: Ellen DeGeneres, Chris Rock, and Billy Crystal, my hometown's undisputed heavyweight comedy champ.

After all the famous comics crack a couple of jokes, an announcer with a big, booming voice reminds everybody that "the winner of the Planet's Funniest Kid Comic Contest will take home one million dollars and come back to Hollywood to star in their very own half-hour sitcom for BNC's exciting new season!"

"Great," says Ray Romano when the announcer is done. "I can see it now. A new sitcom called *Everybody Loves Patty*. Or maybe they all love Antony, or Judy, or Jamie. Hey, how come all four finalists have names that end in an *ee* sound?"

"Because *ee* names are funny," says *Billy* Crystal. "Always have been, always will be."

Chatty Patty (the girl with a double *ee* in her name) goes on first and wows the crowd with her dumb act, still cribbing material from Gracie Allen.

She gets a huge ovation when her fifteen minutes are up.

Once again, America will decide who they think is the funniest kid comic on the planet. They can text or call special numbers to vote. Chatty Patty holds up her index finger to show everybody that she's number one (or to prove that she hasn't been picking her nose).

Antony Guerrero is up next. Like always, he is hysterical. And a little edgy. Tonight, he makes fun of American football.

"Soccer is football. Football isn't. Americans don't play football with their feet unless they're punting. Or running. I guess you have to use your feet to run. But the kickers? The real football players? Come on. They're the skinniest dudes on the team. They wear funny face masks. When they kick the ball through the uprights, nobody screams, 'Fieeeeeeeld goooooooooooooal!'"

Third up is Judy Nazemetz.

Yes. She funny. She should be—she's had joke doctors and comedy coaches working with her at a secret high-tech laugh lab. I think one of her writers must be Tommy Cooper, a famous British comedian and magician who died way back in the eighties, because her set is full of recycled Cooperisms.

I had a great dinner last night at a fancy restaurant. I ordered everything in French, which surprised everybody. It was a Chinese restaurant.

Last night, I dreamed I ate a ten-pound marshmallow. When I woke up, my pillow was gone.

The audience loves her. Me? Not so much. Tommy Cooper told the jokes better. Plus, he didn't play nasty tricks on his so-called friends.

When her fifteen minutes are up, Judy chats with Ray Romano, holds up three fingers to urge everybody to vote for her, and bounds offstage.

It's time for our fourth and final contestant. Yes, in the second half of the second hour, it is finally my turn to roll onstage and spin comedy gold.

There's only one problem.

Nobody can find me.

Chapter 71

WHERE'S JAMIE-O?

Chapter 72

LADIES AND GENTLEMEN, PRESENTING ME!

Sorry about that.

I was off in the wings. Sweating. And saying a quick prayer that what I'm about to do isn't completely dumb or totally insane.

I've decided to risk everything on one story.

My story. No jokes, really. No one-liners.

Just the truth, the whole truth, and nothing but the truth. They say that sometimes, the truth can be funnier than fiction.

I sure hope it is tonight.

I wheel myself to center stage and just let it all come tumbling out.

"Hi, I'm Jamie Grimm. I'm really glad to be here

tonight. You know, a lot of people say that if I don't win this contest, I shouldn't worry. 'Don't let losing get you down, Jamie. You'll be back on your feet in no time.' Really?"

I look down at my legs and my wheelchair.

"Well, if that's true—wow! I kind of hope I lose!"

The audience laughs. They're with me. So I take them on a ride.

"So yeah, I'm in a wheelchair. Haven't always been this way. I used to run around and swim and bounce on a trampoline. I even did the hokey-pokey. Put my right leg in, took it out, put my left leg in, and shook it all about.

"Anyway, after my accident, I moved down to Long Beach and got an after-school job in my uncle Frankie's diner."

"I used to live in Cornwall. A small town in upstate New York. My cousin Stevie still calls me the 'Crip from Cornball' because I'm kind of a hick."

"My cousin Stevie is the biggest bully in my school. But, because I was already in a wheelchair when I moved in, he thinks I cheated him."

But I have great friends at school, too. For one thing, they put up with me. See, after I won a couple of contests, I kind of forgot who I was and turned into a jerk. Okay. There was no "kind of" about it. I became a giant Jerkasaurus. To quote Groucho Marx, I had the brain of a four-year-old boy. And I'll bet he was glad to get rid of it.

"My first time onstage at a comedy club, I nearly drowned in my own flop sweat. Good thing my seat cushion is basically a giant foam-rubber sponge."

This club's indoor sprinkler system seems to be fully functional. However, most clubs put the sprinklers in the ceiling, not some kid's armpits.

"After my uncle Frankie had his heart attack, I dropped out of this competition, and the only reason I'm here right now is because my friend Gilda Gold did a YouTube video of a comedy routine I did in the corridors of Long Beach Middle School."

"So many people kept telling me how good I was and I started to believe them. Did my ego get overinflated? Did I become a first-class jerk? Little bit."

I give America as much of my story as I can squeeze into fifteen minutes. All the stuff you've been reading in these books?

That's my A material, folks.

Because it's my A+ life.

Yeah, some of it is a little corny. Then again, so am I.

Maybe what Stevie Kosgrov says about me is true.

At heart, maybe I'm still just the Crip from Cornball.

Chapter 73

A BACKSTAGE MIRACLE

Did I win?

Well, we won't know until America finishes voting and the golden envelope is opened tomorrow night during a special one-hour super-duper results-show edition of the Planet's Funniest Kid Comic Contest.

That's right. It takes them an hour to open an envelope, pull out a card, and read a name.

But that's okay.

I've already won a pretty amazing prize: The Smileys come backstage after the show, and guess what?

THEY'RE SMILING!

Even more remarkable, Stevie Kosgrov is acting like he is my best and happiest friend in the whole world.

Speech bubble: You people from Long Beach! You're all PHONIES! The kid in the wheelchair walks; you frowny-faced people smile. I'm not signing up any of you!

THE FOLLOWING IS BASED ON A TRUE INCIDENT.

"You were so good," Stevie gushes. "Awesome, even. When you told that joke about me being a bully? Oh, I laughed so hard, tears ran down my legs. Well, tears or *something* wet."

"Um, thanks, Stevie."

"Hey, you wanna go grab an In-N-Out burger with me?"

"That would be fun," says Mr. Smiley, his grin wider than his pants.

"Super-duper funterrific," adds Mrs. Smiley. "Ha hee ho ho!"

"Um," I say, "you guys are just faking it, right?"

Nobody denies it. They all flip their smiles upside down and turn them back into frowns.

"It was a *joke*, Jamie," says Mr. Smiley.

"What's the matter, Cornball?" Stevie laughs. "Don't you have a sense of humor?"

Chapter 7⅞

LUCKY DAY?

The next day is one of the longest of my life.

The votes—over one hundred million were texted or phoned in—are being tabulated. The results show goes on the air, live, at eight o'clock. But the winner won't be announced until 8:55 PM at the earliest.

Everybody has an opinion about who's going to be crowned the Planet's Funniest Kid Comic.

The blogs, newspaper critics, and morning TV shows all seem to think Judy Nazemetz will win. Except the ones that think Antony Guerrero gave the funniest performance. Or the other ones that say Chatty Patty Dombrowski is on her way to taking home one million dollars and starring in her own BNC-TV sitcom.

Yes, all the experts seem to agree on one thing: The winner won't be *me*.

But guess what? My friends and the folks back home in Long Beach have all been calling and texting me for hours.

"You were, without a doubt, the best!" says Pierce.

"You were awesome, dude!" says Gaynor.

"You done good," says Gilda. "Real good."

"You funny!" says Mr. Burdzecki, my favorite Russian customer at Uncle Frankie's diner. "You very, very funny! Funniest on this planet. Mars, too. Even Jupiter. The jokers on Jupiter? *Pah.* They not funny."

They're all behind me one hundred percent. And now that I think about it, none of them ever gave up on me, even when I almost gave up on myself.

I've never loved them more.

Especially Uncle Frankie.

"You were hysterical, kiddo," he says when we have breakfast together. "I loved how you imitated what my face looked like when I had that heart attack. *Aaack!* And don't worry. If, for some bizarro reason, you don't win and don't wind up with your own TV show, you can always be a guest star on mine."

"Huh?"

"I got a call this morning. The Discovery Channel wants me to do a reality show: *Mr. Yo-Yo!*"

Chapter 75

MAY I HAVE THE ENVELOPE, PLEASE? PRETTY PLEASE?

Welcome to the longest fifty-five minutes in history.

We four finalists sit onstage at the Nokia Theatre while Ray Romano and the judges crack jokes and analyze our acts from the night before. They show video clips of our routines. Special musical guests show up and sing songs. They even bring out the dog act that won *America's Got Talent* a few years back.

Finally, mercifully, right before I plop my last available drop of flop sweat onto the floor, Ray Romano starts opening envelopes.

"The person getting the fourth-highest number of votes was…"

Long pause. Long enough for me to realize that Mr. Romano just came up with a very polite way of saying *"And the loser is..."*

I brace myself. Hunker down in my chair. I know he's going to read my name.

But he doesn't.

"Patricia Dombrowski."

Chatty Patty is trying to smile, even though she wants to scream. Or weep. Probably both. I think this is why her cheeks are squirming like a squirrel with a faceful of chestnuts roasted over an open fire.

"The next runner-up," says Ray Romano, "is..."

Another pause. Longer than that last one. My shoulders are so tense they're almost in my ears.

"Antony Guerrero."

I can't believe this.

It's down to Judy Nazemetz and me. She looks at me. I'm looking at her. Her smile is big and fake. Mine is quivering and queasy.

"One more envelope," says Ray Romano. "Inside, we have the name of the winner. See, there's really no need for me to announce the runner-up, because if I did, everybody would know who the winner is, too. Am I right? I mean, we could, I guess, if you really want us to, we could make another envelope and—"

"Yo, Ray!" shouts Chris Rock. "Just tell us who won!"

"Fine. Be that way."

He tears open the envelope. Pulls out a card. "The winner. Of one million dollars and their own TV show on BNC. The Planet's Funniest Kid Comic. Our first champion. Could be our last, too, unless we do this again next year."

Man. Mr. Romano is really good at stretching stuff out.

"The name I'm about to announce, because it is written on this card in a very lovely font…is…"

Pause.

Longest pause ever.

Since the beginning of time.

You could drive a circus train through this pause.

Seriously.

Enough already.

Ray Romano takes a deep breath. My heart shuts down.

Chapter 76

I'M SORRY.
COULD YOU REPEAT THAT?

*J*amie Grimm! *The funniest kid comic on the planet is Jamie Grimm!*"

I won?

O.

M.

G.

This is unbelievable.

The crowd at the theater goes wild.

Somebody hands me a ginormous trophy. Uncle Frankie comes running up onstage and throws his arms around me.

"I always knew you were the funniest kid in the whole wide world!"

Now everybody comes streaming onto the stage to congratulate me. Billy Crystal. Chris Rock. Ellen DeGeneres. Ray Romano. The bestselling author of all time, James Patterson. The Smileys, who are actually smiling for real! Even Stevie, who's probably thinking of my (his) money. A guy lugging a typewriter named Chris Grabenstein (the guy, not the typewriter). Laura Park, who has ink all over her fingers. That crazy kid Rafe Khatchadorian. Even Amanda Durley, who won some kind of contest.

Just like I just did.

Can you believe this?

It's official: I Totally Funniest!

Chapter 77

SAY GOOD-BYE TO HOLLYWOOD!

The next morning, bright and early, I'm ready to leave LA and go home to celebrate my victory with my friends, the ones who have been with me for this whole incredible ride.

Unfortunately, Hollywood isn't quite ready to let go of me.

And it's not just because I'm supposed to start work ASAP on my new TV show, which, by the way, the people at BNC want to call *I Funny TV*.

Nope. The Los Angeles airport is just a big crazy showbiz zoo filled with agents and lawyers and publicists instead of lions and tigers and bears.

Somehow, the Smileys and I make our way to the airport security gate. One look from the tough-looking security guards makes the Hollywood zoo animals finally back off. I'm so grateful I don't even mind when they make me empty all my pockets. My lint collection might have suffered, but that's a small price to pay to be able to go home.

Chapter 78

GOING BACK IN TIME

When we land in New York, I ask Uncle Frankie if we can make a quick side trip to visit some old friends.

"But everybody's waiting for us in Long Beach," he says. "The mayor wants to read you your official proclamation. It's Jamie Grimm Day. I think they give you coupons for ice cream cones when they give you a proclamation. But you'll have to wait until all the ice cream shops are open again."

"That's all great, Uncle Frankie, but, well, this is more important. For me, anyway. None of this would've ever happened without them. They helped me find my funny bone even before you did. Maybe because they're doctors and knew where to look."

Uncle Frankie grins. "Toss that two tons of tin

in the backseat, kiddo, and crank up the doo-wop
music. We're going on a road trip."

We stow my Planet's Funniest Kid Comic trophy
in the backseat of Uncle Frankie's car, text a few
friends in Long Beach to let them know we're
running late, crank up the "sha-boop-bee-boo"
tunes, and drive north to the Hope Trust Children's
Rehabilitation Center in upstate New York.

When I was a patient at the center, we all called
it the Hopeless Hotel, because every single one
of us thought we were hopeless cases until the
doctors, nurses, and physical therapists convinced
us we weren't.

I head for the rehab center's patient library.

When Uncle Frankie and I roll through the door, I see my orthopedic surgeon, Dr. David Sherman. He's standing right in front of the bookshelves crammed with joke books and comedy videos—what he used to call "Jamie Grimm's personal medicine chest."

Every day, either he or one of the nurses or my physical therapist or an orderly would bring me a couple of joke books or funny videos from these very special shelves. Even in my full-body cast, I could read. Even when nobody thought I would live, I could laugh.

Dr. Sherman is the one who always tells his patients "Laughter is the best medicine."

I think he's right.

I think all that laughter kept me alive back then.

I think it's what keeps me smiling now.

"Jamie!" exclaims Dr. Sherman when he sees me. "You were fantastic at the finals! Hilarious. I voted for you. Everybody here did—even the kids wrapped up in more plaster than you ever wore. They just had to ask the nurses and orderlies to do their texting for them!"

"Thank you, Dr. Sherman." I hold up my trophy. "Here. I want you guys to have this."

"But, Jamie…"

"You deserve it. I figure you can use it as a bookend. And a reminder that no matter how serious your situation, jokes can help you feel better. You were so right. Laughter can help you survive anything, no matter how horrible."

"Even Hollywood," quips Uncle Frankie.

You could fill it with gum balls or Skittles. It'll hold a ton.

"Well, thank you, Jamie," says Dr. Sherman. "This library needs a sturdy bookend or two. These last couple of months, we've been adding quite a few new videos to our comedy collection."

"Really?" I say. "What'd you guys get? *Seinfeld* episodes? Charlie Chaplin's silent movies? Classic *Tonight Show*s with Johnny Carson?"

Dr. Sherman smiles and shakes his head.

"Nope. This whole shelf is reserved for our favorite comedian. A funny kid who never, *ever* quit on us. A young guy named Jamie Grimm."

Chapter 79

HOME SWEET HOME

Pretty soon, it's back to the same old same old.

Yes, I might be the Crip from Cornball, but Long Beach on Long Island—with Uncle Frankie, all my friends, tons of memories, and the frowning Smileys (including Stevie Kosgrov)—really feels like home now.

The cleanup after Hurricane Sam is still continuing. The boardwalk is already being repaired.

Everybody in town is pulling together and working on it. Even the zombies and vampires and talking dogs and Godzilla the Garbageman and all the other somewhat strange figments of my imagination are helping out.

Yes, every once in a while, Uncle Frankie (I asked him to be my business manager) and I talk to Joe Amodio from BNC about the *I Funny TV* show I'm going to star in. And now and then, we have to talk to the bankers about how my million dollars are doing. Well, my half a million.

Yes, we spent the other half.

Uncle Frankie is getting a brand-new diner and jukebox. The Smileys are getting a new house, Smileyville 2.

And Uncle Sam is getting a whole bunch of income tax.

As for my half, well…I wish I could say I'll use it for something awesome like a penthouse apartment in New York City with an indoor bowling alley. But Uncle Frankie and the Smileys have told me it's for college and to pay for any medical advancements that might happen down the line.

Who knows? Maybe being funny will eventually help me walk again.

But right now, I'm just back to being in school. Being a kid.

Of course, a lot of folks want to shake my hand, knock knuckles, or slap me a high or low five.

Best part of being home?

Hanging with my buds. Pierce, Gaynor, and Gilda. Everybody wants to shake hands with them, too. Let's face it—they've been a huge part of my journey. I couldn't have done any of this without them, either.

I'm even kind of glad to see Stevie Kosgrov back on his old turf, prowling around in the schoolyard, blocking my path.

It's like déjà vu all over again.

"What?" Stevie sneers at me. "You think I'm going to treat you special just because you're some kind of world-famous comedian in a wheelchair?"

"I sure hope not, Stevie. I just want what I've always wanted: to be treated like everybody else."

"Congratulations, Crip. Your wish is about to come true."

And then he gives my chair a good hard shove and tips me over.

I'm down on the ground, flat on my back. I thrust both arms up over my head and let out a joyous whoop!

"All right!" I shout. "Woo-hoooo! That's what I'm talking about. I'm just a regular kid like the rest of you knuckleheads. Thank you! You've been a great audience. I love you. I love my life. I even love Stevie Kosgrov!"

You know why I always get bullied? I can't stand up for myself! Yes, the world looks different when you see it from butt level. And believe me — crowded elevators smell different to a guy in a wheelchair, too. Come on, folks. It's good to laugh at your problems. Hey, everybody else does. Yep, I'm on a roll!

James Patterson has had more #1 bestsellers for children than any living writer. He is the author of the Middle School, I Funny, Treasure Hunters, and Daniel X novels, as well as *House of Robots*. His blockbusters for adults, featuring enduring characters like Alex Cross—in addition to his many books for teens, such as the Maximum Ride series—have sold more than 300 million copies worldwide. He lives in Florida.

Chris Grabenstein is a *New York Times* bestselling author who has collaborated with James Patterson on the I Funny and Treasure Hunters series and *Daniel X: Armageddon*. He lives in New York City.

Laura Park is a cartoonist and the illustrator of the I Funny series and four books in the Middle School series. She is the author of the minicomic series *Do Not Disturb My Waking Dream*, and her work has appeared in *The Best American Comics*. She lives in Chicago.